W9-ANV-295

DATE DUE			
Oct 29 '81			
Dec 11 '81			
Sep 23 '82			

Books by Joan Didion

A Book of Common Prayer
Play It As It Lays
Run River
The White Album

Published by POCKET BOOKS

Joan Didion

A BOOK OF COMMON PRAYER

PUBLISHED BY POCKET BOOKS NEW YORK

The lines from W. H. Auden's "Lullaby" are excerpted from *Collected Shorter Poems 1927–1957* by W. H. Auden, copyright 1940; copyright renewed © 1968 by W. H. Auden. Reprinted by permission of Random House, Inc.

POCKET BOOKS, a Simon & Schuster division of
GULF & WESTERN CORPORATION
1230 Avenue of the Americas, New York, N.Y. 10020

Copyright © 1977 by Joan Didion

Published by arrangement with Simon and Schuster
Library of Congress Catalog Card Number: 76-50067

ISBN: 0-671-83475-4

First Pocket Books printing February, 1978

10 9 8 7 6

Trademarks registered in the United States and other countries.

Printed in the U.S.A.

ONE

1

I WILL BE HER WITNESS.

That would translate *seré su testiga,* and will not appear in your travelers' phrasebook because it is not a useful phrase for the prudent traveler.

Here is what happened: she left one man, she left a second man, she traveled again with the first; she let him die alone. She lost one child to "history" and another to "complications" (I offer in each instance the evaluation of others), she imagined herself capable of shedding that baggage and came to Boca Grande, a tourist. *Una turista.* So she said. In fact she came here less a tourist than a sojourner but she did not make that distinction.

She made not enough distinctions.

She dreamed her life.

She died, hopeful. In summary. So you know the story. Of course the story had extenuating circumstances,

3

weather, cracked sidewalks and paregorina, but only for the living.

Charlotte would call her story one of passion. I believe I would call it one of delusion. My name is Grace Strasser-Mendana, *née* Tabor, and I have been for fifty of my sixty years a student of delusion, a prudent traveler from Denver, Colorado. My mother died of influenza one morning when I was eight. My father died of gunshot wounds, not self-inflicted, one afternoon when I was ten. From that afternoon until my sixteenth birthday I lived alone in our suite at the Brown Palace Hotel. I have lived in equatorial America since 1935 and only twice had fever. I am an anthropologist who lost faith in her own method, who stopped believing that observable activity defined anthropos. I studied under Kroeber at California and worked with Lévi-Strauss at São Paulo, classified several societies, catalogued their rites and attitudes on occasions of birth, copulation, initiation and death; did extensive and well-regarded studies on the rearing of female children in the Mato Grosso and along certain tributaries of the Rio Xingu, and still I did not know why any one of these female children did or did not do anything at all.

Let me go further.

I did not know why I did or did not do anything at all.

As a result I "retired" from that field, married a planter of San Blas Green coconut palms here in Boca Grande and took up the amateur study of biochemistry, a discipline in which demonstrable answers are commonplace and "personality" absent. I am interested for example in learning that such a "personality" trait as fear of the dark exists irrelative to patterns of child-rearing in the Mato Grosso or in Denver, Colorado. Fear of the dark can be synthesized in the laboratory. Fear of the dark is an arrangement of fifteen amino acids. Fear of the dark is a protein. I once diagrammed this protein for Charlotte. "I don't quite see why calling it a protein makes it any different," Charlotte said, her eyes flickering covertly back to a battered Neiman-Marcus Christmas catalogue she had received in the mail that morning in May. She had reached that stage in her sojourn when she lived for mail, sent away for every catalogue, filled out every coupon, wrote many letters and received some answers. "I mean I don't quite see your point."

I explained my point.

"I've never been afraid of the dark," Charlotte said after a while, and then, tearing out a photograph of a small child in a crocheted dress: "This would be pretty on Marin."

Since Marin was the child Charlotte had lost to history and was at the time of her disappearance eighteen years old, I could conclude only that Charlotte did not care to pursue my point.

Also, for the record, Charlotte was afraid of the dark.

Give me the molecular structure of the protein which defined Charlotte Douglas.

In at least two of the several impenetrably euphemistic "Letters from Central America" which Charlotte wrote during her stay here and tried unsuccessfully to sell to *The New Yorker*, she characterized Boca Grande as a "land of contrasts." Boca Grande is not a land of contrasts. On the contrary Boca Grande is relentlessly "the same": the cathedral is not Spanish Colonial but corrugated aluminum. There is a local currency but the American dollar is legal tender. The politics of the country at first appear to offer contrast, involving as they do the "colorful" Latin juxtaposition of *guerrilleros* and colonels, but when the tanks are put away and the airport reopens nothing has actually changed in Boca Grande. There are no waterfalls of note, no ruins of interest, no chic boutiques (Charlotte went so far as to rent a storefront for one such boutique, but my son Gerardo turned the storefront to his own purposes and it has been since the October Violence a Pentecostal reading room) to provide dramatic cultural foil to voodoo in the hills.

In fact there is no voodoo in the hills.

In fact there are no hills, only the flat bush and the lifeless sea.

And the light. The opaque equatorial light. The bush and the sea do not reflect the light but absorb it, suck it in, then glow morbidly.

Boca Grande is the name of the country and Boca Grande is also the name of the city, as if the place defeated the imagination of even its first settler. At least once each year, usually on the afternoon of the Anniversary of Independence, the Boca Grande Intellectual Union sponsors a debate, followed by a no-host cocktail party, as to who that first settler might have been, but the arguments are desultory, arbitrary. Information is missing here. Evidence goes unrecorded. Every time the sun falls on a day in Boca Grande that day appears to vanish from local memory, to be reinvented if necessary but never recalled. I once asked the librarian at the Intellectual Union to recommend for Charlotte a history of Boca Grande. "Boca Grande has no history," the librarian said, and he seemed

6

gratified that I had asked, as if we had together hit upon a catechistic point of national pride.

"Boca Grande has no history," I repeated to Charlotte, but again Charlotte did not quite see my point. Charlotte was at that time preparing a "Letter" describing Boca Grande as the "economic fulcrum of the Americas." It was true that planes between, say, Los Angeles and Bogotá, or New York and Quito, sometimes stopped in Boca Grande to refuel, and paid an inflated landing fee. It was also true that passengers on such flights often left a dollar or two in the airport slot machines during the time required for refueling, but revenue from an airport landing fee and eighteen slot machines did not seem to me to constitute, in the classical sense, an economic fulcrum.

I suggested this to Charlotte.

Boca Grande exported copra, Charlotte said. Principally your own.

Boca Grande did export copra, principally my own, and, in about the same dollar volume, Boca Grande also exported parrots, anaconda skins, and macramé shawls.

What I was overlooking entirely, Charlotte said, was what Boca Grande "could become."

A "Letter" from a city or country, I suggested, was conventionally understood to be a factual report on that city or country, not as it "could become" but as it "was."

Not necessarily, Charlotte said.

Another of Charlotte's "Letters" covered the "spirit of hope" she divined in the Boca Grande *favelas*. Boca Grande has no *favelas*, even the word is Portuguese. There is poverty here, but it is obdurately indistinguishable from comfort. We all live in cinderblock houses.

7

Charlotte wanted color. By way of color I could tell her only that the Hotel del Caribe was said to have Central America's largest ballroom, but Charlotte was not satisfied with that. Nor with the light.

2

CALL THIS MY OWN LETTER FROM BOCA GRANDE.

No. Call it what I said. Call it my witness to Charlotte Douglas.

One or two facts about the place where Charlotte died and I live. Boca Grande means "big mouth," or big bay, and describes the country's principal physical feature precisely as it appears. Almost everything in Boca Grande describes itself precisely as it appears, as if any ambiguity in the naming of things might cause the present to sink as tracelessly as the past. The Rio Blanco looks white. The Rio Colorado looks red. The Avenida del Mar runs by the sea, the Avenida de la Punta Verde runs by the green point. The green point is in fact green. On reflection I know only two place names in Boca Grande which evoke an idea or an event or a person, which suggest a past either Indian or colonial.

One of these two exceptions is "Millonario."

As in Millonario Province.

So named because our palms grow there and our

copra is milled there, and my husband's father was the rich man, the *millonario,* a St. Louis confidence man named Victor Strasser who at age twenty-three floated some Missouri money to buy oil rights, at age twenty-four fled Mexico after an abortive attempt to invade Sonora, and at age twenty-five arrived in Boca Grande. Upon his recovery from cholera he married a Mendana and proceeded to divest her family of interior Boca Grande.

Victor Strasser died at ninety-five and for the last sixty years of his life preferred to be addressed as Don Victor.

I called him Mr. Strasser.

There is Millonario and there is also "Progreso." In fact there are two Progresos, El Progreso *primero* and El Progreso *otro.* The first Progreso was the grand design of my brother-in-law Luis, the toy of his fifteen-month presidency, his new city, his capital, twenty matched glass pyramids intersected by four eight-lane boulevards, all laid out on fill in the bay and connected to the mainland until recently by a causeway. The matched glass pyramids were never finished but the eight-lane boulevards were. Until a few years ago, when the causeway collapsed, I would take lunch out to the first Progreso and eat there alone, sitting on the site of a projected monument where all four empty boulevards converged. On the fill between the boulevards bamboo grew up through the big Bechtel cranes, abandoned the day Luis was shot. Luis was the last of my brothers-in-law to place himself in so exposed a position as that of *El Presidente.* Since Luis they have tended to favor the Ministry of Defense for themselves, and the presidency for expendable cousins by marriage. In the years after Luis was shot water hyacinths clogged the culverts at Progreso and after rain the boulevards would remain all day in shallow flood, the film of water shimmering with mosquito larvae and with the rainbow slick from rusting oil tanks. Until the collapse I would go out there maybe once a week, and stay most of the afternoon. It occurs to me that I was perhaps the only person in Boca Grande inconvenienced by the collapse of the Progreso causeway.

At some point after the collapse Gerardo took Charlotte to Progreso by boat.

I recall asking Charlotte at dinner if she found Progreso *primero* as peaceful as I did.

Charlotte began to cry.

As for Progreso *otro,* which might have even more radically challenged Charlotte's rather teleological view of human settlement, I have not seen it in some years. Neither has anyone else. This second Progreso was another new city, in the interior, built on leased land (ours) by an American aluminum combine during the bauxite chimera here. (There was bauxite, yes, but not as much as the geologists had predicted, not enough to justify Progreso *otro.*) After the mines closed a handful of engineers stayed on, trying to find some economic use for the aluminous laterite which made up the bulk of the deposit, but one by one they got fever or quit or moved to the combine's operation in Venezuela. The last two left in 1965. The road in, which cost thirty-four million American dollars to build, can still be discerned from the air, quite clearly, a straight line of paler vegetation. My husband wanted to maintain the road, said always that the interior had things we might want access to, but after Edgar died I let it grow over. What I wanted from the interior had nothing to do with access.

*   *   *

Edgar was the oldest of the four sons of Victor Strasser and Alicia Mendana.

It was the brother nearest Edgar's age, Luis, who was shot on the steps of the presidential palace in April 1959.

You will have gathered that I married into one of the three or four solvent families in Boca Grande. In fact Edgar's death left me in putative control of fifty-nine-point-eight percent of the arable land and about the same percentage of the decision-making process in La República (recently La República Libre) de Boca Grande. *El Presidente* this year wears a yachting cap. The two younger Strasser-Mendana brothers, Little Victor and Antonio, the two Edgar and Luis called *los mosquitos,* participate in the estate only via a trust administered by me. Victor and Antonio do not much like this arrangement, nor do their wives Bianca and Isabel, nor does Luis's widow Elena, but there it is. The joint decision of Edgar and his father. *Fait accompli* on the morning Edgar died. There it was and there it is. (A small example of why it is. The day Luis was shot Elena flew to exile in Geneva, a theatrical gesture but unnecessary, since even before her plane left the runway the coup was over and Little Victor had assumed temporary control of the government. The wife of any other Latin president would have known immediately that a coup in which the airport remained open was a coup doomed to fail, but Elena had no instinct for being the wife of a Latin president. Nor does she make a particularly appropriate presidential widow. In any case. A few weeks later Elena came back. Edgar and his father and I met her at the airport. She was wearing tinted glasses and a new Balenciaga coat, lettuce-green. She was carrying a matching parrot. She had not taken this parrot with her from Boca

12

Grande. She had bought this parrot that morning in Geneva, for seven hundred dollars.) In any event there is not as much money in all of Boca Grande as Victor and Bianca and Antonio and Isabel and Elena accuse me of having secreted in Switzerland.

Strike Bianca.

Bianca does not accuse me of having secreted any money in Switzerland because Bianca was taught at Sacre Coeur in New Orleans that discussions of money are not genteel. Also strike Isabel. Isabel does not accuse me of having secreted money in Switzerland because Isabel is so rarely here, and has been told by her doctor in Arizona that discussions of money disturb the flow of transcendental energy.

I continue to live here only because I like the light.

And because I am intermittently engaged by the efforts of my extant brothers-in-law to turn a profit on the Red Cross.

And because my days are too numbered to spend them in New York or Paris or Denver imagining the light in Boca Grande, how flat it is, how harsh and still. How dead white at noon.

One thing at least I share with Charlotte: I lost my child. Gerardo is lost to me. I hear from him regularly, see him all too often, talk to him about politics and new films and the bud rot we are experiencing in the interior groves, but I talk to him as an acquaintance. In Boca Grande he drives an Alfa Romeo 1750. In Paris, where he has lived off and on for fifteen years on a succession of student visas, he rides a Suzuki 500 motorcycle. I always think of Gerardo on wheels, or skis. I like him but not too much any more. Gerardo embodies many of the failings of this part of the world, the rather wishful machismo, the defeating touchiness, the conviction that his heritage must be aristocratic; a general attitude I do not admire. Gerardo is the grandson of two American wildcatters who got rich, my father in Colorado minerals and Edgar's father in Boca Grande politics, and of the Irish nursemaid and the *mestiza* from the interior they respectively married. Still he persists in tracing his line to the court of Castile. On the delusion front I would have to say that Gerardo and Charlotte were well met.

I tell you these things about myself only to legitimize my voice. We are uneasy about a story until we know who is telling it. In no other sense does it matter who "I" am: "the narrator" plays no motive role in this narrative, nor would I want to.

Gerardo of course does play a motive role. I do not delude myself there.

Unlike Charlotte I do not dream my life.

I try to make enough distinctions.

I will die (and rather soon, of pancreatic cancer) neither hopeful nor its opposite. I am interested in Charlotte Douglas only insofar as she passed through Boca Grande, only insofar as the meaning of that sojourn continues to elude me.

3

ACCORDING TO HER PASSPORT, ENTRY VISA, AND International Certificate of Vaccination, Charlotte Amelia Douglas was born in Hollister, California, forty years before her entry into Boca Grande; was at the time of that entry a married resident of San Francisco, California; was five-feet-five-inches tall, had red hair, brown eyes, and no visible distinguishing marks; and had been successfully inoculated against smallpox, cholera, yellow fever, typhus, typhoid, and paratyphoid A and B. The passport had been renewed four months before at New Orleans, Louisiana, and bore entry and departure stamps for Antigua and Guadeloupe, unused visas for Australia and the British Solomon Islands Protectorate, a Mexican tourist card stamped at Mérida, a visa and entry stamp for Boca Grande, and no indication that the bearer had reentered the United States during the four months since the renewal of the passport. Nationality NORTEAMERICANA. Type of Visa TURISTA. Occupation MADRE.

There seemed to me many elusive anomalies on

15

these documents, not the least of them Charlotte Amelia Douglas's decision to enter Boca Grande, but none of these nuances suggested themselves to Victor, Little Victor, who had ordered the passport surreptitiously removed from the Hotel del Caribe safe because its number appeared on a United States Department of State list indicating travelers who were to receive certain special treatment.

4

WHEN CHARLOTTE FIRST CAME TO BOCA GRANDE she was referred to always as *la norteamericana. La norteamericana* had been heard typing in her room at the Caribe all night, *la norteamericana* had woken a doctor at two in the morning to ask the symptoms of infant framboesia. *La norteamericana* had advised the manager of the Caribe that he was derelict in allowing the maids to fill the water carafes from the tap. *La norteamericana* had asked a waiter at the Jockey Club if marijuana was in general use in the kitchen. *La norteamericana* had come downstairs in a thin cotton dressing gown one night when the Caribe generator failed and sat alone in the dark at the ballroom piano until three A.M., picking out with one hand, over and over again in every possible tempo, the melodic line of a single song. This story was told to me by a bell-man at the Caribe, the brother of a woman who cooked for Victor and Bianca, and he tried to hum the song that *la norteamericana* had played over and over again. The song was "Mountain Greenery."

17

In those first few weeks before any of us had met her she seemed to appear only in the evenings. An hour or so after the sunset one could see her walking through the empty casino at the Caribe, nodding pleasantly at the idle croupiers and the national police assigned to the casino, breathing deeply at the windows quite as if fresh air could possibly penetrate the dusty blue velvet curtains that lined the room. She would inspect the tables one by one but did not play. After this ritual turn through the casino she would walk on out through the lobby, her step buoyant, purposeful. Later one could see her eating alone on the porch at the Capilla del Mar or at the Jockey Club, always the same table at the Jockey Club, the table beneath the photograph of the Venezuelan polo team which visited Boca Grande in 1948. She would draw the legs of a spiny lobster between her remarkably white teeth and read the *Miami Herald,* reading the classified as attentively as she read the front page, reading both as avidly and as thoroughly as she ate the spiny lobster.

I saw her at the Jockey Club on a few evenings, and heard about her on others. Like so many works of man in Boca Grande the Jockey Club is less than it seems: an aluminum-sided bungalow with rattan card tables and a menu written in French but translated in the kitchen into ambiguous gumbos based mainly on plantains and rice. Although any traveler could obtain a guest card to the Jockey Club by asking for one at an airline ticket office, not many bothered. There was once a nine-hole golf course, but the greens first went spongy and then reverted to swamp. There was once an artificial lake for swimming, but the lake first became infested with freshwater snails and then with the *Schistosoma mansoni* worms that infest the snails. The lake was not drained until after one of Antonio and

18

Isabel's children suffered gastrointestinal bleeding from what was diagnosed in New Orleans as schistosomiasis. The draining of the artificial lake did not go unremarked upon at the Jockey Club. Elena opposed it. Elena recently resigned from the Jockey Club after the membership, led by Victor, defeated her motion to rename the club Le Cercle Sportif. Elena was born and raised on the Guatemalan coast but favors all things French. Elena's resignation did not go unmarked upon at the Jockey Club.

In short.

The presence at the same table night after night of this conspicuous *norteamericana* was not likely to go unremarked upon at the Jockey Club. Actually it would have been hard to overlook Charlotte Douglas anywhere. There was the extreme and volatile thinness of the woman. There was the pale red hair which curled in the damp heat and stood out around her face and seemed almost more weight than she could bear. There was the large square emerald she wore in place of a wedding ring, there were the expensive clothes that seemed to betray in their just perceptible disrepair (the safety pin that puckered the hem of the Irish linen skirt, the clasp that did not quite close the six-hundred-dollar handbag) some equivalent disrepair of the morale, some vulnerability, or abandon.

And there was that strain of exhibitionism, perverse and sometimes witty until it bloomed too long, and tired the observer. If Charlotte Douglas heard someone speaking English at another table she would invade the conversation, offer suggestions for touring, sights not to be missed. As there were neither any conventional "sights" in Boca Grande nor any tourists, only the occasional mineral geologists or CIA man traveling on one or another incorporeal AID mission, these encounters tended to end in obscurely sexual misunderstandings and bewilderment. After dinner she would walk back to the hotel alone, walking very deliberately, tying and retying a scarf which whipped in the hot night wind, seeming to concentrate on the scarf as if oblivious to the potholes in the sidewalk and the places where waste ran into the gutters. At the Caribe desk she would ask for her messages in a halting but flawlessly memorized Castilian Spanish which the night clerk found difficult to understand. As reported to Victor there were never any messages in any case.

5

UNTIL I LOST A FILLING AND HAD OCCASION TO SEE a dentist in Miami I never knew what *la norteamericana* did during the day. At least one thing she did during the day those first few weeks was this: she went to the airport. She did not go to the airport to catch a plane, nor to meet one. She just went to the airport. She was at the counter of the airport coffee shop the morning I left for Miami, not sitting at the counter but standing behind it, holding a watch in her hand. "I certainly wouldn't think yet," she said to the sullen girl whose space she had arrogated, and she tapped the face of the watch with her fingernail. "Nine minutes more. See for yourself."

The girl stared at Charlotte Douglas a moment and then, without speaking, plunged her index finger into the sugar bowl on the counter. Still gazing at Charlotte she licked the sugar from her finger. In another country she might have gone the extra step, made her point explicit, jammed her grimy finger between *la norteamericana*'s teeth, but the expression of proletarian resentment in Boca Grande remains largely symbolic. The *guerrilleros* here would have nothing to say to this girl in the airport. The *guerrilleros* here spend their time theorizing in the interior, and are covertly encouraged to emerge from time to time as foils to the actual politics of the country. Our notoriously frequent revolutions are made not by the *guerrilleros* but entirely by people we know. This is a hard point for the outsider of romantic sensibility to grasp.

"Gastrointestinal infection is the leading natural cause of death in this country," Charlotte said after a while. She said it in English and did not look at the girl. "If you call it natural."

The girl sucked the last grains of sugar from under her scabbed fingernail and rolled it again in the bowl.

"Which I don't particularly."

When the water for Charlotte Douglas's tea had boiled the requisite twenty minutes she made the tea herself, took it to a table by the window and sat there reading an article on the cultivation of vanilla in *Revista Boca Grande*. She moved her lips slightly and seemed entirely absorbed in what she read. When the Miami plane was called she continued reading *Revista Boca Grande*. She never looked up, or out the window. The next afternoon when I came back from Miami Charlotte Douglas was sitting at the same table reading the same copy of *Revista Boca Grande*. It did not occur to me that day that I would ever have reason to consider Charlotte an outsider of romantic sensibility. In any case I am no longer sure that she was. Possibly this is the question I am trying to answer.

Once I knew Charlotte I realized that although she spoke Spanish she had trouble reading it, and tended to lose the sense of even the simplest newspaper story somewhere in the first paragraph, but it could not have mattered in this case since she had no interest in the cultivation of vanilla.

Or in the reform of the Boca Grande tax structure.

Or in the contradiction inherent in a Central American common market.

All of which topics, and others, Charlotte Douglas read about in the Boca Grande airport, her concentration apparently passionate, her expression miming comprehension, here a nod of approval, there a moue of disagreement; her eyes scanning the Spanish words as if she understood them.

When there was nothing else to read.

When, say, the *Miami Herald* did not come in and she had already committed to memory the revised schedules of all five airlines chartered to land at Boca Grande.

6

THE STATE DEPARTMENT LIST ON WHICH CHARLOTTE Douglas's name and passport number appeared stated simply that the United States Embassy should be advised of the entry, the departure, the arrest, the hospitalization, or the participation in civil disorder of anyone listed. Various forms were provided for this purpose, but the immigration officer in charge of the list had mislaid them; as far as he could remember Charlotte Douglas was the only person on the list ever to enter Boca Grande. Victor himself had never before heard of the list, had seen it for the first time when the immigration officer's report on Charlotte Douglas arrived on his desk at the Ministry of Defense, and he regarded the thin leaflet with the eagle on the top page as a mesmeric challenge to his powers of deduction. The list animated a slow week for Victor. The list was a code Victor could not crack. The list so obsessed Victor that he had even solicited Antonio's opinion as to whether those listed were politically suspect, criminal, indigent, or very important.

"Scratch indigent," I suggested.

"The little brother suggested indigent."

Victor routinely referred to Antonio as "the little brother," I think in a stab at ironic distance. Antonio was at that time Minister of Public Works, whatever "Public Works" mean in Boca Grande.

"I don't think indigent," I said.

"Then what?"

"Show me the list."

"The list is for official eyes only."

"You won't show me the list, how should I know 'what.' Ask Bradley."

"I'm asking you."

"I'm not the American ambassador, Victor, Bradley is."

Victor sucked at his teeth and drummed his glossy fingernails on a Steuben paperweight Bradley had given him as a gesture of ambassadorial good will. Victor believed the pale moons of his fingernails to be evidence of noble blood and had a manicurist meet him every day at noon to shape his cuticles and perform other services characterized by Elena as beyond Bianca's range. Elena's faith in the sexual virtuosity of working women was touching and childlike. If I did not completely misapprehend Victor the cuticles came first.

"Ask Bradley," I repeated. "Call the Embassy and ask Bradley."

"We don't run this country at Bradley's convenience."

Put a Strasser-Mendana behind a desk and you have a *tableau vivant* of the famous touchiness of command. Antonio once urinated on the foot of an Italian newspaperwoman who suggested that Boca Grande was perhaps not ready to join the nuclear club. Victor was

25

displeased with Bradley because the week before Bradley had allowed his wife to leave one of Victor's official lunches in the courtyard at three-thirty, before the food was served, pleading faintness from the heat. Victor felt insulted by Americans who grew faint before lunch, even Americans who were, as Ardis Bradley was, forty-four years old and seven months pregnant.

"In any case." Victor studied his nails. "In fact. Bradley is in Caracas."

In any case in fact Bradley was not in Caracas, I had seen him the night before, but it was a theme of Victor's that Tuck Bradley neglected Boca Grande for livelier capitals.

"About those four o'clock lunches in the courtyard," I said.

"I wasn't aware we were talking about any four o'clock lunches in the courtyard."

"Just one detail. While I think of it. Pass it on to Bianca. I don't think the baba au rhum should be out in the sun from twelve-thirty on."

Victor said that he had not called me into his office for advice on serving baba au rhum.

I asked if he had called me into his office to admire the new 380 Mauser automatic pistol mounted on his desk.

Victor snapped his fingers. The aide at the door sprang to my chair and bowed.

"As another *norteamericana* you could meet her," Victor said as I got up. He did not look at me. That he continued this conversation at all confirmed his obsession with the list, because it was past noon. At noon exactly his car always took him to meet his manicurist at the apartment he kept in the Residencia Vista del Palacio. The Residencia was only a block and a half from the Ministry but Victor fancied that his car, a black Mercedes limousine with the license BOCA GRANDE 2 (Victor always allowed *El Presidente* the BOCA GRANDE 1 plate), was the discreet way to go. "In the most natural way you could meet this woman. You could ask her for a coffee. Or a drink."

"Or a baba au rhum."

Victor swiveled his chair to face the window. Many of my visits to Victor's office at the Ministry ended this way, and still do, although the office is now Antonio's. I suppose Isabel is pleased that the office is finally Antonio's but Isabel is spending her usual season at the private hospital her doctor operates in Arizona.

When it was reported to Victor that Charlotte Douglas went to the airport every day he construed immediately that her presence on the list had to do with Kasindorf and Riley. Kasindorf was Bradley's cultural attaché at the Embassy and Riley was a young man who ran an OAS "educational" office called "Operación Simpático" downtown. The connection with Charlotte Douglas, transparent to Victor, was that Kasindorf and Riley also went to the airport every day, met there for coffee at precisely seven-thirty A.M., a time which coincided with the arrival of the night Braniff from Mexico.

In fact Kasindorf and Riley went to the airport not because of the night Braniff from Mexico but because they assumed correctly that Victor had microphones in their offices.

In fact Charlotte Douglas just went to the airport.

7

La norteamericana told a story about playing hide-and-seek with Marin among the thousand trunks of the Great Banyan at the Calcutta Botanical Garden. It had been "the most lyrical" day. She and Marin had "devoured" coconut ice for lunch. She and Marin had wandered beneath the Great Banyan at noon and stayed until after dark.

She leaned toward Victor and me as if the end of the story were a secret never before revealed. "And when Leonard finished his meeting and couldn't find us at the Hilton he was wild, he had people combing Calcutta for us, it was hilarious."

The absence of banyan trees at the American Embassy reminded Charlotte Douglas of this story.

She told a story about sitting in the rain in a limousine at Lod Airport eating caviar with an Israeli general. They had "devoured" the caviar from the tin

28

with their fingers and pieces of unsalted matzoh. The Israeli and Leonard could meet only between planes and the Israeli had brought the caviar.

Again she leaned toward us. "And when Leonard saw the Iranian seal on the tin he wouldn't eat the caviar, and the general said 'don't be a fool, don't make me go to war for it,' it was hilarious."

The absence of caviar at the American Embassy Christmas party reminded Charlotte Douglas of this story.

She talked constantly. She talked feverishly. She talked as if Victor had released her from vows of silence by walking up to where she stood with Ardis Bradley and offering her a crab puff. Every memory was "lyrical," every denouement "hilarious," and sometimes "ironic" as well. Her face was flushed but she was not drunk: she stood very straight and refused even the weak rum punches the Bradleys favored for general entertainments. She seemed to be receiving these pointless but bizarrely arresting stories out of some deep vacuum of nervous exhaustion, transmitting them dutifully in a voice soft and clear and oddly confidential. She used words as a seven-year-old might, as if she had heard them and liked their adult sound but had only the haziest idea of their meaning, and she also mentioned names as a seven-year-old might, with a bewildering disregard for who was listening. "Leonard," she would say, as if we would naturally know who Leonard was, as if the Minister of Defense of a Central American republic and his *norteamericana* sister-in-law, acquaintances of an hour in the crush of an official reception, were of course privy to all the people and places in her life.

There was "Leonard."

There was "Warren."

There was "Marin."

There was the house on California Street in San Francisco and there were the meetings in Calcutta and La Paz and in limousines at Lod Airport.

There were the hotel suites, always "flooded with flowers."

There was the missed plane and its happy ending: Air Force One.

"Imagine Leonard on Air Force One." She had one of those odd intimate laughs that seemed simultaneously to include everyone within hearing and to exclude all possibility of inquiry. "Ardis. Tell them. You know Leonard."

"Actually I don't quite," Ardis Bradley said.

"For that matter imagine Leonard on a camel," Charlotte Douglas said.

"Leonard," Victor said tentatively, looking at Ardis Bradley. "Leonard would be her—"

"Actually I think Tuck might know him," Ardis Bradley said. Ardis had spent twenty years in places like Sierra Leone and Boca Grande and Chevy Chase learning to go look for Tuck when she did not want to answer a question. "Actually I don't want Tuck to miss this."

"Leonard on that camel." Still laughing Charlotte Douglas touched Victor's arm. "After lunch one day in Kuwait."

Victor had the look of someone who had waded out too far. Ardis Bradley had vanished. I was myself unclear as to why this Leonard declined Iranian caviar in one story and lunched in Kuwait in another.

"The inevitable five-course lunch. In the inevitable Valerian Rybar dining room. Followed by the inevitable camel. I tried to postpone the camel part, I kept eating and eating, everything had this vile mint taste, I kept trying to distract the sheikh, I kept asking him what I could—"

She broke off abruptly and shrugged.

"What you could—?"

"It was hilarious." She was looking around the room as if unsure how she had gotten there. "I used to like mint but I don't any more, do you?"

"You kept asking the sheikh what you could—?"

"I suppose it's one of those abandoned tastes. As opposed to acquired. Mint." She focused on Victor with difficulty. "I kept asking the sheikh what I could send him from America. Of course."

"And then," Victor prompted.

"He wanted eight-track cassettes and flowered sheets." Her voice was absent. "They all do."

"But after lunch?"

"After lunch?"

"The camel?"

"The *camel*." She seemed relieved to be handed the thread to her story but had lost interest in telling it. "So Leonard rode the camel. Of course. Leonard had to ride the camel."

"Leonard would be—"

"You know how the Kuwaiti are."

"Your husband? Leonard would be your husband?"

"One of them." Her voice was still absent. "I mean they lay on a camel, you have to ride the camel."

"And he has occasion to travel a great deal." Victor was not to be deflected. "Your husband. Leonard. He travels. For business. For pleasure. For whatever."

"He runs guns," Charlotte Douglas said. "I wish they had caviar."

Victor stared at her.

She speared a shrimp, dipped it in mayonnaise and offered it to Victor. Victor made no response.

"I don't mean literally." She spoke with disinterested patience and still held out the shrimp to Victor. "I don't mean he literally buys and sells the hardware."

"The hardware," Victor said.

She ate the shrimp herself and seemed about to drop the toothpick into the six-hundred-dollar handbag with the broken clasp when Tuck Bradley appeared. To my astonishment she handed Tuck Bradley the toothpick. To my further astonishment he stood there holding it, between two fingers, looking prissy and foolish. Beyond handing him the toothpick Charlotte seemed entirely unaware of Tuck Bradley's presence. "He's kind of a lawyer," she said finally. "He's kind of a lawyer in San Francisco."

"If you're talking about Leonard he's a very well-known lawyer," Tuck Bradley said.

"In a way," Charlotte said.

"In San Francisco," Tuck Bradley said.

"And in some other places," Charlotte said.

And then, her animation returning, she again touched Victor's arm in that way she had of physically touching strangers, of reaching out unconsciously and then drawing back as if she had just realized the gesture's sexual freight; that mannerism, that tic, that way of barely suggesting impossible intimacy. She did this only to strangers but she did not do it to all strangers. I never saw her do it to a woman and I never saw her do it to Antonio. She never did it to Gerardo either but that was because Gerardo did it first, to her. Sexual freight was another area in which I would have to say that Gerardo and Charlotte were well met.

"You know what you need here," she said to Victor, lifting her fingers from his arm as if burned. "You know what Boca Grande needs."

"We're making great headway with the People-to-People program," Tuck Bradley said. "Leaps and bounds."

Neither Charlotte nor Victor looked at him.

"I know what you need here," Charlotte said.

"What do I need here," Victor said. His voice was almost hoarse. "Say it."

She studied the square emerald on the hand that had touched Victor and slid it up and down. She seemed aware of nothing she was doing. She was reflexively seductive. I did not want to watch this happening. I did not want to think of Victor and this woman in the apartment in the Residencia Vista del Palacio and I did not want to see the black Mercedes limousine with the BOCA GRANDE 2 plates parked outside the Caribe.

"Think of what made Acapulco," she said finally. "Think of what turned Acapulco around overnight."

Victor stared at the emerald as if transfixed.

Tuck Bradley snapped the toothpick in two.

I looked away.

"I'm not sure Mrs. Douglas realizes the problems," Tuck Bradley said.

"Think," Charlotte repeated.

"Say it," Victor repeated.

"A film festival," Charlotte Douglas said.

"You won't want the details but it's rather a tragic situation," Ardis Bradley said. "Tuck could tell you better than I."

"I won't bore you with the details but it's rather an interesting situation," Tuck Bradley said. "Don't ask her about her daughter."

I could not have asked Charlotte Douglas about her daughter in any case because Charlotte Douglas had already left, with Victor. I went as planned to Victor's and ate with Bianca, alone. The black Mercedes limousine with the BOCA GRANDE 2 plates was seen first at the Residencia Vista del Palacio and later at the Caribe. Bianca did not then and does not now go out, nor does she express interest in her husband's arrivals and departures. That is another example of the genteel behavior Bianca was taught at Sacre Coeur in New Orleans.

The next afternoon when I saw Charlotte Douglas arguing with the pharmacist in the big drugstore on the Avenida Centrale she did not look at me. She looked disheveled and unwell, her eyes puffy beneath dark glasses, her bright hair unkempt and only partly covered by a bandana.

"You tell me chloromycetin." The pharmacist slapped the counter with his palm. "I give you chloromycetin."

"This is tincture of opium."

"Different type chloromycetin."

"I can smell it, it's opium."

"Same thing. *Para la disentería.*"

"But they're not the same thing at all." Even in her distress she seemed determined to instruct him on this point. "They're both *para la disentería,* but they're quite different. Chloromycetin is a—"

"I give you chloromycetin."

34

"Forget the whole thing," she said, her voice low and her eyes averted from where I stood.

Later that afternoon I sent a maid to the Caribe with twenty chloromycetin and a note asking Charlotte Douglas to have dinner when she was recovered.

8

"CHARLOTTE DOUGLAS IS ILL," I SAID AFTER CHRIST-
mas lunch in the courtyard at Victor and Bianca's.

No one had spoken for twenty minutes. I had timed
it. I had counted the minutes while I watched two
mating flies try to extricate themselves from a melting
chocolate shaving on the untouched Bûche de Noël.
The children had already been trundled off quarreling
to distribute nut cups to veterans, Gerardo had already
made his filial call from St. Moritz, Elena had already
been photographed in her Red Cross uniform and had
changed back into magenta crepe de chine pajamas.
Isabel had drunk enough champagne to begin crying
softly. Antonio had grown irritable enough with Isabel's
mournful hiccups to borrow a pistol from the guard at
the gate and take aim at a lizard in the creche behind
Bianca's fountain. Antonio was always handling guns,
or smashing plates. As a gesture toward the spirit of
Christmas he had refrained from smashing any plates
at lunch, but the effort seemed to have exhausted his
capacity for congeniality. Had Antonio been born in

other circumstances he would have been put away early as a sociopath.

Bianca remained oblivious.

Bianca remained immersed in the floor plan for an apartment she wanted Victor to take for her in the Residencia Vista del Palacio. Bianca had never been apprised of the fact that Victor already had an apartment in the Residencia Vista del Palacio. For five of these twenty minutes it had seemed to me up in the air whether Antonio was about to shoot up Bianca's creche or tell Bianca about the Residencia Vista del Palacio.

"I said *la norteamericana* is sick."

"Send her to Dr. Schiff," Antonio muttered. Dr. Schiff was Isabel's doctor in Arizona. "Let the great healer tell *la norteamericana* who's making her sick."

Victor only gazed at the sky. I did not know whether Victor had seen Charlotte Douglas since the night he took her from the Embassy to the Residencia but I did know that a Ministry courier had delivered twenty-four white roses to the Caribe on Christmas Eve.

"So is Jackie Onassis sick," Elena said. Elena was leafing fretfully through a back issue of *Paris-Match*. "Or she was in September."

"So am I sick," Isabel said. "I need complete quiet."

"I should think that's what you have," Elena said.

"Not like Arizona," Isabel said. "I should have stayed through December, Dr. Schiff begged me. The air. The solitude. The long walks, the simple meals. Yoghurt at sunset. You can't imagine the sunsets."

"Sounds very lively," Elena said without looking up. "I wonder if Gerardo knows Jackie Onassis."

"If that's the *norteamericana* Grace is talking about I think she had every right to marry the Greek," Bianca

37

said. "Not that I would ever care to live in Athens. I wonder about the view from the Residencia."

"Grace was talking about a different *norteamericana,* Bianca." Victor leaned back and clipped a cigar. "Of no interest to you. Or Grace."

"This *norteamericana* is of interest only to Victor." Antonio seemed to be having trouble drawing a bead on the lizard. "But she could tell you about the view from the Residencia. She's an expert on the view from the Residencia. Victor should introduce you to her."

"I don't meet strangers," Bianca said. "As you know. I take no interest. Look here, the plan for the eleventh floor. If we lived up that high we'd have clear air. No fevers."

"Almost like Arizona," Elena said. "I wonder if Gerardo knows Jacqueline de Ribes."

"Arizona," Isabel said. "I wonder what Dr. Schiff is doing today."

Antonio fired twice at the lizard.

The lizard darted away.

Two porcelain wise men shattered.

"Eating yoghurt in the sunset I presume," Elena said.

"Dr. Schiff doesn't believe in guns," Isabel said.

"What do you mean exactly, Isabel, *'Dr. Schiff doesn't believe in guns'?"* Antonio thrust the pistol into Isabel's line of sight. "Does Dr. Schiff not believe in the 'existence' of guns? *Look* at it. *Touch* it. It's *there. What does Dr. Schiff mean exactly?"*

Isabel closed her eyes.

Elena closed the copy of *Paris-Match.*

Bianca began to gather up the fragments of porcelain.

Victor looked at me and spoke very deliberately. "There's no longer any need for you to see the *norteamericana,* Grace. An extremely silly woman."

38

"But then so is your manicurist," Elena murmured.

"If I could live on the eleventh floor I think I'd take an interest again," Bianca said.

"Quite frankly it's better when you don't," Isabel said, abruptly and unsettlingly lucid, and in the silence that followed she stood up and put her arms around Bianca.

For a moment two of my three sisters-in-law stood there in the courtyard with the guard at the gate on Christmas afternoon and buried their faces in each other's shoulders and stroked each other's hair. Only their silence suggested their tears. They were little sisters crying.

Elena rubbed at a drop of champagne on her magenta crepe de chine pajamas.

Antonio drummed his nails on the table.

"It might be better if you left," Victor said to Antonio.

"Maybe I'll go get your *norteamericana* to sit on my face," Antonio said to Victor.

Victor smoked his cigar and looked at me. *"Feliz Navidad,"* he said after a while.

Here is what Charlotte Douglas was said by Elena to have done with the twenty-four white roses Victor sent her on Christmas Eve: left them untouched in their box and laid the box in the hallway for the night maid.

9

"IT'S DEPRESSING TO BE SICK IN A HOTEL."

"I don't mind it." She said it as a child might, and she said nothing more.

"At Christmas."

"I didn't mind."

I tried again. "You're at the mercy of the maids."

"They're very nice here."

I watched Charlotte Douglas unwrap a cracker and fold the cellophane into a neat packet. She had insisted that we meet not at my house but at the Capilla del Mar, that I be her guest.

"Actually I'm never depressed." The act of saying this seemed to convince her that it was so, and she picked up the wine list in a show of resolute conviviality. "Actually I don't believe in being depressed. It's hard to keep wine in this climate, isn't it? Wine and crackers?"

Through two courses of that difficult dinner she never mentioned Victor.

She guided every topic to its most general application.

40

She talked as if she had no specific history of her own.

No Leonard.

No Warren.

As dessert was served she mentioned Marin for the first time: she said that she preferred the Capilla del Mar to the Jockey Club because the colored lights strung outside the Capilla del Mar reminded her of the Tivoli Gardens, where she had once flown with Marin for the weekend. Her face came alive with pleasure as she described this adult's dream of a weekend a child might like, described the puppet shows, the watermills, the picnics with the child. They had made dinners of salami and petits fours. They had scarcely slept. They had wandered beneath the colored lights until Marin's heels blistered, and then they had taken off their shoes and wandered barefoot.

"And when we got back to the hotel we ordered cocoa from room service." Charlotte Douglas leaned across the table. "And I let Marin place the order and tip the waiter and I taught her how to wash out her underwear at night."

I asked if her husband had gone to Copenhagen on business, but she said no. Her husband had not gone to Copenhagen at all. She had just woken up one morning in the house on California Street and decided to fly Marin to Copenhagen. "To see Tivoli. I mean before she was too old to like it."

Her eyes were fixed on the colored lights strung over our table on the porch at the Capilla del Mar. The lights at the Capilla del Mar were not Christmas lights but souvenirs of the season I married Edgar in São Paulo, the season a deranged Haitian dentist convinced the Minister of Health to string the entire city of Boca Grande with a web of colored lights as a specific against typhoid. The red and blue strings mostly shorted out in the first rain, leaving the city in the evening bathed in a necrotic yellow. So it was the night Edgar and I first arrived in Boca Grande from São Paulo. Edgar took me directly to Millonario and left me there until the epidemic waned. When I next saw the city many people had died and the rest seemed immune and the only lights left were at the Capilla del Mar.

I mentioned this to Charlotte.

"That's very interesting," Charlotte said politely, her eyes still on the lights. She had been smoking a cigarette as I talked and there was no ashtray and now, instead of just tossing the cigarette over the porch railing, she flicked off the lighted head with her fingernail, stripped the paper with the same fingernail and crumbled the tobacco neatly into the loam of a potted plant. I had seen men do this often and I had seen women do it in the field but I had never before seen a woman in a beige silk St. Laurent dress do it in a restaurant which passed for fashionable, and the casual dispatch with which Charlotte Douglas did it seemed at distinct odds with her rather demented account of the trip to Copenhagen. "By the way," she said then. "Marin and I are inseparable."

Some weeks later Charlotte again mentioned the weekend she had taken Marin to see Tivoli before she was too old to like it. She said that because Marin had run a fever all weekend, a reaction to her smallpox vaccination, they had never left the Hôtel Angleterre. She had obtained a doctor who was very understanding and nice. The manager at the Angleterre had been very understanding and nice and had sent Marin a marzipan carousel to make up for not seeing Tivoli. In any case it had rained all weekend.

One of two things was true: either Charlotte had gone with Marin to the Tivoli Gardens or Charlotte had wanted to go with Marin to the Tivoli Gardens.

Type of Visa TURISTA. Occupation MADRE.

10

THE NEXT TIME I SAW CHARLOTTE DOUGLAS SHE grabbed up a chicken on the run and snapped the vertebrae in its neck. I had taken her to the annual picnic for the children of the workers in the Millonario groves and the men were killing chickens with machetes but Charlotte's kill was clean. There was no blood. She killed this chicken as efficiently and reflexively as she had field-stripped the cigarette at the Capilla del Mar.

"All the children have red shoes," she said to me and Elena as she handed the dead chicken to the man who had been trying to catch it. She had only smiled vaguely at the man's attempt to congratulate her. She seemed entirely unaware that for a guest of the *dueña* to kill a chicken with her hands was at Millonario an event worth remark. Even Elena had forgotten her sulky pique at being in Millonario and was staring at Charlotte, speechless.

"Red cardboard patent-leather shoes," Charlotte said. "All of them. Why do the children wear red shoes?"

"That chicken," Elena said.

"I mean you see them all over the tropics. Those red shoes."

"How exactly did you kill that chicken?" Elena said.

"Not the right way at all, actually." Charlotte's expression did not change. "Actually they're better if you bleed them live. Marin wanted a pair of red shoes once. When she was six. She cried, I wouldn't buy them."

Charlotte looked away and lifted the hair off her neck.

"I did have a baby who had red shoes," she said after a while. She stood up then and rinsed her hands in a ditch and when she straightened up she dried her hands on her skirt and gazed for a long time at the men still killing chickens with machetes. "You ought to tell them, chickens are better if you bleed them live. There was no reason not to buy Marin those shoes."

Nationality NORTEAMERICANA.

11

A GOLD CIGARETTE LIGHTER ENGRAVED "D.N.C. Atlantic City '64."

A letter of introduction from the Wells-Fargo Bank in San Francisco to the Banco de la República, collapsed two regimes back.

A California drivers' license, recently expired, and credit cards from American Express, Gulf Oil, the Ochsner Clinic in New Orleans, I. Magnin and Saks Fifth Avenue.

$26 American and an equivalent amount in local currency.

An unsealed envelope addressed only to a post-office box in Buffalo, New York. An unfinished letter describing the resemblance of the Capilla del Mar to the Tivoli Gardens.

Two lipsticks, one broken pencil, a folded envelope containing four sulfathalidine and two salt tablets, a vial containing a scent predominantly gardenia, a fortune-cookie tape printed "A surprise is in store for someone you love," and a frayed clipping of one day's horoscope from *Prensa Latina*.

This is a list of the items said to be in Charlotte Douglas's possession (and later returned to the manager of the Hotel del Caribe) at the time of her death in the Estadio Nacional. The square emerald she wore in place of a wedding ring was neither listed nor returned. I took the gold cigarette lighter to Marin in Buffalo but Marin said she had no interest in the past. I do.

TWO

1

THE WIND IS UP TONIGHT.

Palm fronds clatter.

Shutters bang against the sills but I cannot close the windows because the house smells of cancer. Gerardo is somewhere over the sea, due home on the midnight Air France. When I think of the sea here tonight I imagine the water abruptly receding, then swelling back in the tidal surge, *la marejada,* drowning the sea wall, silencing the dogs, softening my burning skin and rinsing my brittle hair and floating the Liberian tanker in the harbor across the submerged boulevards of Progreso *primero.*

Sand-strewn caverns cool and deep
Where the winds are all asleep.

Wishful thinking.

La marejada will not come tonight, nor will I die tonight.

All that will happen tonight is that the generator will fail as usual and I will sit in the dark reciting

Matthew Arnold as usual and when Gerardo arrives from the airport I will pretend to be asleep.

Again as usual.

Since Charlotte's death Gerardo and I have had to learn how to make conversation by day and avoid it in the dark, how to pretend together that my indifference to his presence derives from my being asleep, or in pain, or hallucinating. I am not in such pain that I hallucinate but other people prefer to think that I am. When I speak above a whisper Gerardo and Elena and Victor and Antonio avert their eyes. Even Isabel and Bianca avert their eyes. Even the dim Mendana cousin they brought in from Millonario to nurse me averts her eyes, and crosses herself every time I vomit or ask for a rum-and-quinine or suggest that she is repeating herself. This particularly tedious Mendana was trained as a Sister of Mercy, left the order in 1944 but continues to wear her full habit around Millonario and at family deathbeds, and fancies herself the dispatch-rider between the rest of us and heaven. When I interrupt her accounts of local miracles on the third telling she consoles herself by dismissing me as *"de afuera,"* an outsider. I am *de afuera.* I have been *de afuera* all my life. I was *de afuera* even at the Brown Palace Hotel. It is a little more than a year now since Charlotte Douglas's death and almost two years since her arrival in Boca Grande.

Charlotte Douglas's death.

Charlotte Douglas's murder.

Neither word works.

Charlotte Douglas's previous engagement.

Some of what I know about Marin Bogart's disappearance I know from Charlotte. Some of it I know from Leonard Douglas. Some of it I know from having once seen Warren Bogart and some of it I know from having once seen Marin but most of what I know, the most reliable part of what I know, derives from my training in human behavior.

I do not mean my training under Kroeber at California, nor with Lévi-Strauss at São Paulo.

I mean my training in being *de afuera*.

Nothing I know about Marin's disappearance comes from the "pages" Charlotte apparently wrote during her first weeks in Boca Grande, the pages she was heard typing at night in her room at the Caribe, the pages given to me with her other personal effects by the manager of the Caribe. On those pages she had tried only to rid herself of her dreams, and these dreams seemed to deal only with sexual surrender and infant death, commonplaces of the female obsessional life. We all have the same dreams.

2

THE MORNING THE FBI MEN FIRST CAME TO THE house on California Street Charlotte did not understand why. She had read newspaper accounts of the events they recited, she listened attentively to everything they said, but she could make no connection between the pitiless revolutionist they described and Marin, who at seven had stood on a chair to make her own breakfast and wept helplessly when asked to clean her closet.

Sweet Marin.

Who at sixteen had been photographed with her two best friends wearing the pink-and-white candy-striped pinafores of Children's Hospital volunteers, and had later abandoned her Saturdays at the hospital as "too sad."

Soft Marin.

Who at eighteen had been observed with her four best friends detonating a crude pipe bomb in the lobby of the Transamerica Building at 6:30 A.M., hijacking a P.S.A. L–1011 at San Francisco Airport and landing

54

it at Wendover, Utah, where they burned it in time for the story to interrupt the network news and disappeared.

Marin.

Or so the two FBI men tried to tell Charlotte.

Marin who had eaten coconut ice beneath the Great Banyan at Calcutta.

Marin who had been flown to Copenhagen to see the lights at Tivoli.

Marin who was at that moment, even as the two FBI men occupied Leonard's Barcelona chairs, even as the fat FBI man toyed with one of Leonard's porcelain roses and even as the thin FBI man gazed over Charlotte's head at the 10′ by 16′ silk screen of Mao Tse-tung given to Leonard by one of the Alameda Three, skiing at Squaw Valley.

Or so Charlotte tried to tell the fat FBI man.

The thin one did not seem to be listening.

I am talking here about a day in November one year before the day in November when Charlotte Douglas first appeared in Boca Grande.

One amplification. Some of what Charlotte said about the months which followed Marin's disappearance she did not even say to me. She said it to Gerardo.

I would call that the least reliable part of what I know.

Three or four things I do know about Charlotte.

As a child of comfortable family in the temperate zone she had been as a matter of course provided with clean sheets, orthodontia, lamb chops, living grandparents, attentive godparents, one brother named Dickie, ballet lessons, and casual timely information about menstruation and the care of flat silver, as well as with a small wooden angel, carved in Austria, to sit on her bed table and listen to her prayers. In these prayers the child Charlotte routinely asked that "it" turn out all right, "it" being unspecified and all-inclusive, and she had been an adult for some years before the possibility occurred to her that "it" might not. She had put this doubt from her mind. As a child of the western United States she had been provided as well with faith in the value of certain frontiers on which her family had lived, in the virtues of cleared and irrigated land, of high-yield crops, of thrift, industry and the judicial system, of progress and education, and in the generally upward spiral of history. She was a *norteamericana.*

She was immaculate of history, innocent of politics. There were startling vacuums in her store of common knowledge. During the two years she spent at Berkeley before she ran away to New York with an untenured instructor named Warren Bogart, she had read mainly the Brontës and *Vogue,* bought a loom, gone home to Hollister on weekends and slept a great deal during the week. In those two years she had entered the main library once, during a traveling exhibition of the glass flowers from Harvard. She recalled having liked the glass flowers. From books Warren Bogart gave her to read when she was twenty Charlotte learned for the first time about the Spanish Civil War, memorized the ideological distinctions among the various PSUC brigades and POUM militia, but until she was twenty-two and Warren Bogart divined and corrected her misapprehension she believed that World War II had begun at Pearl Harbor. From Leonard Douglas she had absorbed a passing fluency in Third World power, had learned what the initials meant in Algeria and Indochina and the Caribbean, but on a blank map of the world she could not actually place the countries where the initials were in conflict. She considered the conflict dubious in any case. She understood that something was always going on in the world but believed that it would turn out all right. She believed the world to be peopled with others like herself. She associated the word "revolution" with the Boston Tea Party, one of the few events in the history of the United States prior to the westward expansion to have come to her attention. She also associated it with events in France and Russia that had probably turned out all right, otherwise why had they happened.

A not atypical *norteamericana*.

Of her time and place.

It occurs to me tonight that give or take twenty years and a thousand miles Charlotte Douglas's time and place and my time and place were not too different.

Some things about Charlotte I never understood. She was a woman who grew faint when she noticed the blue arterial veins in her wrists, could not swim in clouded water, and once suffered an attack of acute terror while wading in water where an artesian well churned up the sand. Yet during the time she was in Boca Grande I saw her perform a number of tasks with the same instinctive lack of squeamishness I had seen that day at Millonario. I once saw her skin an iguana for stew. I once saw her make the necessary incision in the trachea of an OAS field worker who was choking on a piece of steak at the Jockey Club. A doctor had been called but the OAS man was turning blue. Charlotte did it with a boning knife plunged first in a vat of boiling rice. A few nights later the OAS man caused a scene because Charlotte refused to fellate him on the Caribe terrace, but that, although suggestive of the ambiguous signals Charlotte tended to transmit, is neither here nor there. Similarly, during the cholera outbreak that year Charlotte volunteered to give inoculations, and she did, for thirty-four hours without sleeping, until the remaining Lederle vaccine was appropriated by one of Victor's colonels. When the colonel suggested that as a *norteamericana* she might be in a position to buy back some of the vaccine Charlotte only smiled, took off the white smock she had borrowed from the clinic, and dropped it at the colonel's feet. For the rest of that day Charlotte sat on the edge of the Caribe pool with her feet in the water and stared at the birds circling in the white sky. She did not wear dark glasses and by five o'clock the pale skin around her eyes was burned and puffy. For a few days Charlotte spoke to Gerardo about leaving Boca Grande, but within a week she had revised the incident to coincide with her own view of human behavior and assured me that the vaccine had been taken only so that the army could lend its resources to the inoculation program. I used to think that the only event in Charlotte Douglas's life to resist her revisions and erasures was Marin's disappearance.

"Interesting portrait there," the thin FBI man said, his eyes still on the 10′ by 16′ silk screen given to Leonard by one of the Alameda Three.

"Warhol," Charlotte said.

"I would have guessed Mao."

"Mao. Of course." Charlotte had no idea how one of the Alameda Three had happened to come by a Warhol silk screen. Or maybe it had not been one of the Alameda Three at all, maybe it had been one of the Tacoma Eleven or some Indian or Panther or heir to a motion-picture studio, Charlotte could never keep Leonard's clients straight. They came in packs and they ate and they asked for odd drinks and they went through her medicine cabinet and they borrowed and did not return her sweaters and they never addressed her directly and she could never remember their names. She wished that she could. She also wished that Marin would walk through the door of the house on California Street with a tow ticket tied to her windbreaker.

"You see you don't know Marin," she added finally.

"I know her."

The fat FBI man coughed. The other examined a matchbox he had picked up from a table.

"I mean I'm her mother."

"Of course you are," the fat FBI man said.

"I don't quite follow what she's saying about this Chinese couple," one of the new FBI men said. It was almost time for lunch and Charlotte had not yet eaten breakfast and the house on California Street seemed to be filling with men who spoke to each other as if Charlotte were not there. "What Chinese couple."

"The Chinese couple who come to the house," Charlotte repeated. "And do the Peking duck."

"I don't quite follow what she's talking about."

"She's talking about caterers, Eddie, it's not a point."

"Maybe if she could run through it again. Marin arrives from Berkeley. Start there. Day before yesterday. Approximately twenty hours prior to the bombing. Marin arrives from Berkeley to—"

"To borrow a windbreaker." Charlotte spoke by rote. "To go skiing."

"To borrow a windbreaker. But she doesn't leave right away. She goes up to her room and she's up there alone maybe three, four hours, ballpark figure, you aren't sure which. Up in her room she—"

"You wanted her to tell it, Eddie, let her tell it."

Charlotte raised her voice. "She went through some things in her drawers."

"What things?"

"I don't know what things. She's eighteen years old, I don't go through her drawers.'"

"Mrs. Douglas mentioned a gold bracelet, Eddie, don't forget the gold bracelet."

"You mentioned a gold bracelet, Mrs. Douglas."

"I said she found a gold bracelet she thought she'd lost."

"In a drawer."

"In a drawer, behind a drawer." There was something about the gold bracelet Charlotte wanted not to think about. Marin had dropped the bracelet on the kitchen table and told Charlotte to keep it. Marin had called the bracelet "dead metal." Charlotte wished suddenly that she had not mentioned the bracelet and she also wished suddenly that Leonard were not in Nicosia. Or Damascus. Or wherever he was. He had written out the cities and the hotels and the telephone numbers on a legal pad upstairs but Charlotte had not looked at it since he left. Her left temple was beginning to hurt and she resented the FBI men for remembering the gold bracelet.

"Now we get to the part where I call the Chinese couple and ask them to do the Peking duck." She could hear the edge in her voice but could not control it. "All right?"

"We're back to the Chinese couple, Eddie."

"Caterers," the man the others called Eddie said.

"Not exactly," Charlotte said.

"They come to your house? They cook dinner?" Charlotte nodded.

"Then they're caterers. Wasn't that kind of an exceptional thing to do, Mrs. Douglas, telephoning these caterers?"

"I don't quite see the exceptional part." Charlotte

wished that the FBI man would not insist on calling the Chinese couple "caterers." They were not caterers, they were a couple. Under certain circumstances which had not yet arisen they might come to the house on California Street not as cooks but as guests. Charlotte knew a lot of couples like the Chinese couple who did the Peking duck. She knew the Algerian couple who did the couscous, she knew the Indonesian couple who did the rijsttafel, she knew the Mexican couple who were actually second-generation Chicano but who did the authentic Mexican dinner, not common enchiladas and refried beans but exquisite recipes they had learned while vacationing at the Hotel Inglaterra in Tampico. She knew the Filipino couple, she knew the Korean couple. She had recently uncovered the Vietnamese couple. In the kitchen of the house on California Street these and other couples regularly reproduced the menus of underdeveloped countries around the world, but usually for twelve or twenty-four people. Charlotte had never before called one of these couples to cook for fewer than twelve. This time she had. That might be the exceptional part. She began to see calling the Chinese couple to do Peking duck for herself and Marin in a different light, a light not necessarily more revealing but different.

In this light the gold bracelet she had made Marin take had been too loose on Marin's wrist.

In this light Marin had been too thin and pale for a child who skied and played tennis and was supposed to have spent the week before celebrating Thanksgiving off Cabo San Lucas.

In this light Charlotte had lit the fire and turned on the record-player and called the Chinese couple for the same reason she had insisted that Marin take the bracelet: to keep Marin from the harm outside.

"I mean a catered dinner for two must be quite an expensive proposition," the FBI man said.

"They're quite reasonable." Charlotte spoke automatically. "Considering."

"Catered dinner for *one*," the FBI man said. "Technically. Since Marin didn't stay."

"Marin had a paper to finish before she went skiing, I told you." Charlotte avoided the blank gaze of the FBI men. "She had a paper to finish for her seminar in I think *Moby Dick*."

The fat FBI man spoke for the first time since the arrival of the others. "She's not registered as a student, Mrs. Douglas, I suppose you know that."

"Actually you should try this couple." Charlotte spoke very clearly to shut out his voice. She did not know why she had said it was a seminar in *Moby Dick*. Marin had never mentioned any seminar in *Moby Dick*.

"She hasn't been registered for two quarters, and the quarter before that she took all incompletes, but I'm sure you know this."

"I mean if you like Cantonese food at all."

Moby Dick had something to do with Warren.

At nineteen Charlotte had written a paper on Melville and Warren had failed her. Warren had failed her and had rung her doorbell for the first time at midnight with the paper torn in half and a bag of cherries and a bottle of bourbon and they had not left the apartment for forty-eight hours. For the first three she called him Mr. Bogart and for the next forty-five she called him nothing at all and it was not until the third day, when he took her to his apartment and asked her to clean it up and she came across the letter from the department chairman advising him that his contract would not be renewed, that she ever called him Warren.

Still not looking at the FBI man Charlotte stood up and began placing their coffee cups on a tray.

"They also do a marvelous Szechuan beef thing."

The fat FBI man signaled the others to leave the room.

"Marin's father taught a seminar in *Moby Dick* once," Charlotte said before she broke.

After the FBI men left that morning Charlotte went upstairs to Marin's room. The Raggedy Ann Warren had sent for Marin's twelfth birthday was on its shelf. The teddy bear Warren had sent for Marin's fourteenth Easter was on its chair. The guitar once used by Joan Baez was on the windowseat, where it had been since the night Leonard bought it for Marin at an ACLU auction. The embroidered Swiss organdy curtains were as pristine as they had been the day Marin picked them out. The old valentines beneath the glass on the dressing table were unchanged, the tray of silver bangles and bath oil and eye shadow untouched. All that Marin had removed from the room was every picture, every snapshot, every clipping or class photograph, which contained her own image.

3

ONE IMAGINES A SWEET INDOLENT GIRL, SOFT WITH baby fat, her attention span low and her range of interests limited. Marin approved of infants and puppies. Marin disapproved of "meanness" and "showing off." She appeared to approve equally of Leonard and Warren, and tailored her performance to please each of them. When Warren came to San Francisco she would appear instinctively in the navy-blue blazer no longer required by the progressive Episcopal day school she attended. For Leonard and his friends she would wear blue jeans, and a *dashiki* which scratched her skin. On principle she "adored madly" the presents Warren occasionally sent, although by her fifteenth birthday these presents still ran to the sporadic stuffed animal in a box bearing the charge-plate stamp of whatever woman he was living with at the time. In principle she was tolerant of Leonard's efforts on the behalf of social justice, although in practice she often found the beneficiaries of these efforts "weird" and their predicaments "unnecessary." That Episcopal day school Marin attended from the age of four until she entered Berkeley had as its aim "the development of a realistic but optimistic attitude," and it was characteristic of Charlotte that whenever the phrase "realistic but optimistic" appeared in a school communiqué she read it as "realistic and optimistic."

That was Charlotte.

Not Marin.

Marin would never bother changing a phrase to suit herself because she perceived the meanings of words only dimly, and without interest. Perhaps because of her realistic but optimistic attitude Marin was easily confused by such moral questions as were raised by the sight of someone disfigured (would a good God make ugly people?) or the problem of dividing her Halloween candy with the Episcopal orphans (do six licorice balls for the orphans equal one Almond Hershey for Marin, if Marin dislikes licorice?), and when confused could turn sulky, and withdrawn.

What else do I know about Marin.

I know that her posture toward all adult women was agreeably patronizing.

I know that her posture toward all adult men, toward Leonard and toward Warren and toward any man at all who was not disfigured, was uncomplicatedly seductive. Her mind was empty of grudges and hurts and family malice. Her energies were simple and physical and in the summertime her blond hair had the cast of pale verdigris from the chlorine in swimming pools. Charlotte adored her, brushed her pale hair and licked the tears from her cheeks, held her hand crossing streets and wanted never to let go, believed that when she walked through the valley of the shadow she would be sustained by the taste of Marin's salt tears, her body and blood. The night Charlotte was interrogated in the Estadio Nacional she cried not for God but for Marin. Gerardo told me that. I prefer not to know who told Gerardo.

"I SEE," LEONARD KEPT SAYING FROM WHEREVER HE was on the day the FBI first came to the house on California Street. "I see."

"I don't see," Charlotte said. "Frankly I don't see at all."

There was a silence. "You're calling from the house."

"What difference does it make."

Charlotte could hear only the faint crackle on the cable. Actually she had forgotten that she was never supposed to call Leonard from the house if she had anything important to tell him. She was supposed to lose any possible surveillance and place the call on what Leonard called a neutral line. During the Mendoza trial in Cleveland she had called Leonard every day from a pay phone in Magnin's and once she had taken a room in a motel on Van Ness just to call London and tell Leonard that she missed him, but now that she had to tell him that Marin was said to have bombed the Transamerica Building she was calling from the white Princess phone in Marin's room.

"I mean what difference could it possibly make if they're listening, since I'm only telling you what they told me in the first place."

Still Leonard said nothing.

"I mean," Charlotte said, "I can't leave the house."

"I want you to leave the house. I want you to stay with Polly Orben in Sausalito. I want you to call Polly Orben right away——"

"I don't want to stay with Polly Orben." Polly Orben had been Leonard's analyst for eight years. Charlotte did not know what Polly Orben and Leonard had been talking about for eight years but Polly Orben frequently reported that they were within a year or so of "terminating," or "ending." She seemed to mean finishing the analysis. "I don't want to leave the house."

"It's Wednesday, Polly counsels at Glide on Wednesday, call her at Glide——"

"I have to be here when Marin calls."

"My point is this." Leonard spoke very carefully. "You don't know where Marin is."

"That's exactly why I have to be here."

"And if you don't know where Marin is, then you can't *tell* anyone where Marin is. Under oath. Can you."

Charlotte said nothing.

"If you see my point."

Still Charlotte said nothing.

"Get in touch with Warren. Tell him exactly what I just told you. Tell him he doesn't want to hear from her."

"I guess I'll just wait here and perjure myself," Charlotte said finally. "And then hire you."

Charlotte did not call Polly Orben at Glide. Charlotte did not get in touch with Warren. For the rest of that lay Charlotte only lay on Marin's bed, staring at the black-button eyes of the Raggedy Ann Warren had sent for Marin's twelfth birthday. Charlotte did not see how Marin could have played any useful role in flying an L–1011 to Wendover, Utah. Marin could not even drive a car with a manual transmission.

Marin could not fly an L–1011 so Marin must be skiing at Squaw Valley.

Marin had called her great-grandmother's wedding bracelet dead metal.

Marin had been in bed with the flu on her twelfth birthday and as if she were four instead of twelve had slept all night with Warren's Raggedy Ann in her arms.

When it began to rain at six o'clock Charlotte wrapped herself in Marin's blanket but did not close the windows. She went downstairs only once, when two of the FBI men came back to ask if she had a recent photograph of Marin.

"I don't know." In a drawer upstairs she had three recent photographs that Marin had overlooked but there was some quite definite reason why she did not want the FBI men to have them. She could not put her finger on the reason but she knew that there was one. "I'd have to look."

She made no move to look.

She realized suddenly that she was still holding the Raggedy Ann, with its dress pulled up to show the red heart that said I LOVE YOU.

One of the FBI men cleared his throat.

"I don't suppose you've heard from her," he said finally.

"I'm sure you'd tell us if you had," the other said.

She wanted to slide the Raggedy Ann behind a pillow but she was sitting in one of Leonard's Barcelona chairs and there were no pillows.

"Actually I wouldn't," she said finally.

"Mrs. Douglas—"

"Actually I'd lie. I'd lie to you and I'd perjure myself in court. You know that. You heard me tell my husband that on the telephone."

The two FBI men looked away from each other.

"Or if you didn't hear me *someone* in your office certainly did, you should compare notes down there." She did not want to talk to the FBI this way but she could hear her own voice and it sounded bright and social and it did not stop. "Someone down there's been listening to me on the telephone for at least five years, you should know me by now. I'd lie."

"I'm sure you know that under the law a parent has no special—"

The other FBI man held up his hand as if to silence his partner.

"Maybe you'd like someone to stay with you tonight, Mrs. Douglas. Keep an eye on things."

"I *have* someone keeping an eye on things. I have all those people you moved into the apartment across the street. Haven't I. I mean I didn't see you move them in, but I know how you operate." She could not seem to stop herself. It was the Raggedy Ann. She resented their catching her with the Raggedy Ann. "One thing I *don't* know. I don't know if you kept tapes of all those telephone calls."

Neither man spoke.

"I mean it could be very useful if you did. If you could sit down now and listen to those telephone calls you'd probably know more about Marin and me and Leonard and Warren than I even remember. You could probably figure the whole thing out."

One of the men closed his briefcase. The other reached for his raincoat.

"You must have six or seven hundred hours on Marin and Lisa Harper alone. Doing their algebra." Charlotte smoothed the Raggedy Ann's dress over its red heart and did not look at the FBI men. "Lisa's at Stanford this year. In case you missed the installment when Lisa got into Stanford and Marin didn't."

"We're not on opposing sides, Mrs. Douglas."

"Marin cried when the letter came from Stanford. You probably remember that. Marin crying."

The next morning when Charlotte woke in Marin's bed the rain was streaming down Marin's organdy curtains and puddling on the parquet floor. Charlotte knew as she woke why she could not give the FBI a recent photograph of Marin. She could not give the FBI a recent photograph of Marin because any photograph useful to them would show Marin's eyes, and then Marin's eyes would stare back at her from newspapers and television screens, and she was not yet ready to deliver her child to history.

Another day passed and still Charlotte did not place a call to Warren. It was not possible to actually "call" Warren: it was necessary instead to "place a call" to Warren, to leave messages at various offices and apartments he frequented around New York and wait for him to call back. Usually he called back between one and three A.M. San Francisco time, or four and six A.M. New York time.

"Where's your interesting Jew husband," Warren would say if Charlotte did place the call and he did call back. He would say this if Charlotte had placed the call to say that Marin had a cold and he would say this if Charlotte had placed the call to say that Marin was going to tennis camp and he would also say this if Charlotte were to place a call to say that Marin was wanted by the FBI.

"I'm calling about something important," she would say.

She knew what she would say because she knew what he would say.

"I said where's your interesting Jew husband," he would say.

"Leonard is not Jewish. As you know. I'm calling—"

"There's nothing wrong with being 'Jewish.' As you say. Has he made an anti-Semite out of you along with everything else?"

"I have to tell you—"

"All you 'have to tell' me is where the well-known radical lawyer is. Come on. Admit it. He's at Bohemian Grove, isn't he. He's . . . let me get it right, he's *making the revolution at Bohemian Grove.*"

She would not place a call to Warren just yet.

In any case Warren could not learn about Marin from the FBI because the FBI would not know how to place a call to Warren.

In any case there was no need to place a call to Warren because Marin was skiing at Squaw Valley.

In any case Leonard would place the call to Warren.

Charlotte settled many problems this way.

Leonard flew home immediately but because of an airport strike at Beirut and a demonstration at Orly it took him thirty-six hours to arrive in San Francisco, and by then they had sifted the debris and identified Marin's gold bracelet attached like a charm to the firing pin of the bomb. They had also received the tape, and released Marin's name to the press. Charlotte learned about the tape when she opened the door of the house on California Street and found a television crew already filming. On the six o'clock news there was film that showed Charlotte opening the door, turning from the camera and running upstairs as a young Negro pursued her with a microphone. When this film was repeated at eleven it was followed for the first time by the picture of Marin, the famous picture of Marin Bogart, the two-year-old newspaper picture of Marin in her pink-and-white candy-striped Children's Hospital volunteer's pinafore. The newspaper had apparently lost the negative and simply cropped and enlarged a newsprint reproduction in which Marin was almost indistinguishable, clearly a complaisant young girl in a pinafore but enigmatically expressionless, her eyes only smudges on the gravure screen. In the weeks that followed the appearance of the picture those two photogravure smudges would eradicate every other image Charlotte had of Marin's eyes. The day I finally saw Marin I was surprised by her eyes. She has Charlotte's eyes. She has nothing else of Charlotte's but she has Charlotte's eyes.

5

YOU NO DOUBT HEARD THE TAPE.

"This is not an isolated action. We ask no one's permission to make the revolution."

I heard only part of it, on a Radio Jamaica relay, but I read excerpts from it in *Time* and in *Prensa Latina* and in the *Caracas Daily Journal,* excerpts always illustrated by the impenetrable picture of the child in the candy-striped pinafore. I heard only part of the Radio Jamaica relay because Gerardo was at the house the night it was played, and he had arranged the evening as usual to annoy and discomfit everyone involved. I used to think the design of such evenings Gerardo's only true amusement.

Or more accurately his only true vocation.

Since he was only fitfully amused by anything at all.

In the first place Gerardo had asked Elena to come for dinner that night. That Elena came was a tribute to Gerardo's sexual power over her, because Elena was not speaking to me. Elena was not speaking to me because I had that morning advised her that she and

74

Gerardo would be better off exhibiting their tedious interest in each other's bodies in the Caribe ballroom than at political meetings under surveillance by both Victor and the Americans. I did not like hearing about Elena and Gerardo from Tuck Bradley. I did not like Tuck Bradley hearing about Elena and Gerardo from Kasindorf and Riley. As a matter of fact I had already heard about Elena and Gerardo, from Victor, and I did not like that either.

Elena said that Gerardo was the only person in the entire family who understood dancing or "fun."

I said that this might be true but in this case Gerardo's "fun" lay not in dancing but in embarrassing the family by parading the widow of a family *presidente* at meetings of people opposed to the family. It made no difference if Gerardo went to these meetings, because Gerardo's image in the community, deserved or not, was that of someone "worthless," and "young." It did make a difference if she, Elena, went to these meetings, because her image in the community, again deserved or not, was that of someone "virtuous," and "older."

A national treasure as it were.

But Elena had stopped speaking. Elena did not even know that these events to which Gerardo took her were "meetings." She believed them to be "parties." I think she still does.

In any case.

In the second place.

Just asking Elena to dinner had not quite sated Gerardo's craving for social piquancy. He had asked Elena and then he had proceeded to ask an extremely sullen girl he had been seeing off and on for years, an ambitious *mestiza* who had once gone to Paris with him and left him first for a minor Thyssen and then for an English rock-and-roll singer and had recently returned to Boca Grande to redeploy her resources. The girl was the daughter of the cashier at the Jockey Club and her name was Carmen Arrellano but she called herself Camilla de Arrellano y Bolívar and did not visit the Jockey Club. On this particular evening she was sulking because Gerardo was listening to the radio, and possibly also because I had told the cook to ignore her demand to be served a separate dinner of three boiled shrimp on a white plate with half a lemon wrapped in gauze. The cook had found this demand particularly offensive because her son was married to Carmen Arrellano's cousin.

"All class enemies must suffer exemplary punishment."

The voice on Radio Jamaica was sweetly instructive.

"When the fascist police think we are near we will be far away. When the fascist police think we are far away we will be near."

"She lisps," Gerardo said.

"She sounds like those Cubans at the party," Elena said. Elena had several times mentioned this "party" to which she and Gerardo had gone the night before, apparently thinking to annoy me and Carmen Arrellano in a single stroke. "Doesn't she, Gerardo. Those dreadful Cubans who came with Bebe Chicago. I don't mean the lisp, I mean the words."

"I'm only listening for the lisp," Gerardo said. "I wouldn't mention Bebe Chicago in front of Grace if I were you, she'll cut off your clothes allowance."

I said nothing. Bebe Chicago was a West Indian homosexual who after some years at the London School of Economics and a few more organizing Caribbean "liberation fronts" out of Mexico had turned up in Boca Grande to see what he could promote.

His name was François Parmentier but everyone called him Bebe Chicago. I have no idea why. He was said to have connections with the *guerrilleros*. I heard about him frequently, from both Victor and Tuck Bradley. People like Bebe Chicago come and go in Boca Grande, and the main mark they leave is to have provided inadvertent employment for the many other people required to follow them around and tap their telephones.

"Grace thinks Bebe Chicago and I are using you," Gerardo said.

"Delicious," Elena said. "Do it."

"Actually that's not the dynamic." Gerardo smiled at me and Elena. "Actually I'm using Bebe Chicago. Listen to this girl. I like the lisp and the pinafore together. Very nice."

"All you think about is sex," Elena said.

"You wish that were true," Gerardo said. "But it's not."

"She bores me," Carmen Arrellano said sullenly. Carmen had been arranged since dinner in a corner of the room where she could gaze at herself in a mirror. "It bores me."

"Of course it bores you," Gerardo said. "You don't like sex. You can't dress for it, there are never any photographers. Or is that what bores you?"

"The *radio*," Carmen said sullenly.

"I didn't dream you were listening," Elena said. "I thought you were devising a new makeup. Have you ever thought of bleaching your eyebrows?"

"I said this is boring me," Carmen said to Gerardo.

Gerardo held up a hand to silence her and moved closer to the radio.

"This was really a terribly amusing party you missed last night," Elena said to Carmen.

Carmen picked up a magazine.

"Steel band," Elena said. Actually Elena had not found the "party" amusing at all. Actually Elena had complained before she stopped speaking to me that Gerardo's friends did not dance but sat around a filthy room watching a Cuban film about sugar production. Elena smiled at Carmen. "Lots of Dominicans and these frightful Cubans. We danced until five this morning. Are you still bored?"

"Carmen is always bored," Gerardo said. "Excuse me. *Camilla* is always bored. I want to hear this lisp."

"We shall reply to repression with liberation. We shall reply to the terrorism of the dictatorship with the terrorism of the revolution."

Elena continued to smile benignly at Carmen.

Carmen dropped her magazine on the floor and stood up.

"We're tiring your mother," Carmen announced to Gerardo. "And your amusing aunt."

"I should say," Elena said. "It's nearly nine."

"I'll take you home when this is over," Gerardo said. "Meanwhile you might listen."

"Pinched little parrot talking about capitalism," Carmen said. "Who cares about capitalism."

"That's very interesting, Carmen." Gerardo was turning the radio dials to keep the relay from fading. "It's very interesting because there's a body of thought that capitalism is precisely what ruined your character."

There was a silence.

Elena giggled.

"Also yours," Gerardo said to Elena. "Not that I agree entirely."

I was relieved when the relay faded out.

I was equally tired of listening to Gerardo and

78

Elena and Carmen Arrellano and the little girl on the tape.

I recall that none of the four had my sympathy that night.

THE NIGHT CHARLOTTE FIRST HEARD THE TAPE SHE apparently tried to transcribe it word for word, so that she could explain to Leonard and Warren what Marin had in mind. She got only as far as the part where Marin discussed what she called the revolutionary character of her organization. *"Now I would like to discuss the revolutionary character of our organization,"* Marin definitely said on the tape. *"The fact that our organization is revolutionary in character is due above all to the fact that all our activity is defined as revolutionary."*

Charlotte read this sentence several times. She wondered if she had misheard Marin, or missed an important clause. The tape was still running and Marin could still be heard, talking about "expropriation" and "firepower" and "revolutionary justice" and about how the Transamerica Building was one of many symbols of imperialist *latifundismo* in San Francisco, but Charlotte was still fixed on that one sentence. *The fact that our organization is revolutionary in character is due above all to the fact that all our activity is defined as revolutionary.* She could parse the sentence but she could make no sense of it, could find no way to re-phrase it so that Leonard and Warren would understand.

As it turned out she did not need to explain the sentence to Leonard because when he arrived from the airport at midnight he said that the sentence was not original with Marin but had been lifted from a hand-book by a Brazilian guerrilla theorist named Marighela.

"I've got just one thing to say about the operation," Leonard said.

Charlotte waited.

"I know where they got their rhetoric but I'd like to know where they got their hardware."

As it turned out Charlotte did not need to explain the sentence to Warren either because when he called from New York at two that morning he had already heard the tape and, like Leonard, he had just one thing to say about the operation.

"Fuck Marin," he said.

I think Warren Bogart would have had my sympathy that night.

WHEN I MARRIED EDGAR STRASSER-MENDANA I RE-
ceived, from an aunt in Denver who had been taken as
a bride to a United Fruit station in Cuba, twenty-four
Haviland dessert plates in the "Windsor Rose" pattern
and a letter of instructions for living in the tropics. I
was to allow no nightsoil on my kitchen garden, boil
water for douches as well as for drinking, preserve my
husband's books with a thin creosote solution, schedule
regular hours for sketching or writing and regard the
playing of bridge as an avoidance of reality to be in-
dulged only at biweekly intervals and never with de-
depressive acquaintances. In this regime I could perhaps escape what the letter called the fever and disquiet
of the latitudes. That I had been living in these same
latitudes unmarried for some years made no difference
to my aunt: she appeared to locate the marriage bed as
the true tropic of fever and disquiet.

So in many ways did Charlotte.

As it happens I understand this position, having
observed it for years in societies quite distant from San

Francisco and Denver, but some women do not. Some women lie easily in whatever beds they make. They marry or do not marry with equanimity. They divorce or do not. They can leave a bed and forget it. They sleep dreamlessly, get up and scramble eggs.

Not Charlotte.

Never Charlotte.

I think I have never known anyone who regarded the sexual connection as quite so unamusing a contract. So dark and febrile and outside the range of the normal did all aspects of this contract seem to Charlotte that she was for example incapable of walking normally across a room in the presence of two men with whom she had slept. Her legs seemed to lock unnaturally into her pelvic bones. Her body went stiff, as if convulsed by the question of who had access to it and who did not. Whenever I saw her with both Victor and Gerardo it struck me that her every movement was freighted with this question. Who had prior claim. Whose call on her was most insistent. To whom did she owe what. If Gerardo's hand brushed hers in front of Victor her face would flush, her eyes drop. If she needed a bottle of wine opened on those dismal valiant occasions when she put on her gray chiffon dress and tried to "entertain" she could never just hand the corkscrew to Gerardo. Nor could she hand the corkscrew to Victor. Instead she would evade the question by opening the wine herself, usually breaking the cork. I recall once telling Charlotte about a village on the Orinoco where female children were ritually cut on the inner thigh by their first sexual partners, the point being to scar the female with the male's totem. Charlotte saw nothing extraordinary in this. "I mean that's pretty much what happens everywhere, isn't it," she said. "Somebody cuts you? Where it doesn't show?"

I keep those cuts that don't show in mind when I think about Charlotte Douglas's passage from the house on California Street to the Boca Grande airport. Charlotte Amelia Douglas. Charlotte Amelia Bogart. Born Charlotte Amelia Havemeyer. Charlotte. I am not even certain she was talking figuratively.

In the first week after the release of Marin's tape these events occurred.

Charlotte received a call from a young woman in New York who said that Warren would arrive in San Francisco on a midnight plane. Warren did not.

Charlotte received a call from a spiritualist in the Netherlands who said that he perceived the aura of a girl in a pinafore selling tripe in the Belleville section of Paris. He would discuss his vision in detail upon receipt of a first-class airplane ticket to San Francisco, round-trip and refundable.

Leonard received a call from the sister of a convict at San Quentin who said that her brother had reason to know that Marin was working as an aide in a state mental hospital. He would name the state upon receipt of an unconditional parole.

The young woman in New York called back to say that Warren had missed the midnight plane but would arrive in San Francisco the next afternoon. Warren did not.

A pair of FBI men came for coffee every morning.

An apartment-court manager on the outskirts of Detroit told NBC that he had seen Marin and "two jumped-up coloreds" loading carbines into the trunk of a 1957 Pontiac at dawn in the Livonia Mall parking lot. By the time he appeared on CBS he described

Marin's companions as "possibly black or Indian" and the car as a 1957 Pontiac "or some later-model General Motors vehicle." In the *Detroit Free Press* the story was headlined "A SEARCH FOR A NERVOUS INDIAN."

Marin was said to be in Havana.

Marin was said to be in Hanoi.

Warren left two messages on the answering service that he would definitely arrive in San Francisco via TWA the following morning at 10:35 A.M. He did not.

"What have we here," Leonard said when he finally walked into the room Charlotte had taken in the Fairmont Hotel. Leonard had addressed a bar luncheon on constitutional law at the Fairmont and a telephone had been brought to the dais and it was Warren calling from New York. Charlotte had watched Leonard take the call from Warren and then she had left the dais and gone to the desk and asked for a room and telephoned Leonard to meet her upstairs when he finished lunch. The room was cold and the radiator jammed off and the big windows overlooking the Pacific Union Club would not close. Yet for an hour and ten minutes Charlotte had been sitting barefoot in the gray afternoon light wearing only the handmade navy-blue silk underwear she had just bought in a shop in the lobby. She had been trying not to remember about Marin or Warren. She had been trying to remember a carnal mood.

"No. Don't tell me," Leonard said. "Let me guess. You decided the way to avoid seeing Warren was to move to the Fairmont."

"I don't want to talk about Warren," Charlotte said. "I got him a ride out."

"Don't talk about him," Charlotte said. "Come here."

"I know perfectly well what you're doing. Even if you don't."

"Don't talk about it. Don't laugh. I just want it."

"You don't want it at all."

Charlotte sat on the edge of the bed and pulled the spread around herself. "I did."

"You're transparent, Charlotte. To everyone but yourself."

Charlotte gazed out the window. "Somebody died," she said after a while. "Somebody died at the Pacific Union Club. While you were talking. Downstairs."

"How do you know."

"The fire department came. The resuscitator squad. And then an ambulance. And they lowered the flag."

Leonard sat on a chair facing the bed. "I know exactly what you're trying to do."

"Look. You can see the flag. Half mast. What do you mean, you got him a ride out?"

"Never mind Warren. It's a lousy idea, Charlotte, trying to have a baby."

"Who said anything about a baby? I say I want to fuck, you say I don't. You say you got Warren a ride out, I say how, you say never mind Warren. I say somebody died at the Pacific Union Club, you start talking about having a baby. I don't know what you're talking about."

Leonard kept his eyes on Charlotte but she did not meet them.

"Quite honestly I don't."

"Quite honestly I don't think you do. Quite honestly I always know what you're thinking before you do. What you're thinking now is this: you get yourself pregnant, Warren can't get to you. ABC. QED. Don't ask me why. Where did you get that underwear?"

Charlotte said nothing.

"Has it ever occurred to you that your primary erogenous zone is your underwear?"

Charlotte had pulled the bedspread closer and smoked a cigarette without speaking and there had not seemed any point in staying in the cold room after that. In the elevator it occurred to her that he had been trying to make her laugh with him but that was another mood she could not remember. In fact she did want a baby.

"He apparently called the office and gave Suzy a lot of shit before he got me here." Leonard nodded at the Fairmont doorman. " 'Your friend *Warren*,' Suzy calls him."

"I don't want him to come out here."

"It's not up to you, Charlotte. Come out of your trance. He wants to come out."

"Then why hasn't he."

"You know as well as I do *why hasn't he*, Charlotte, he hasn't been able to promote an airplane ticket, that's *why hasn't he*."

"He didn't say that."

"Of course he didn't say that. Wake up."

Charlotte concentrated on trying to tie her scarf in the wind.

"So as soon as the Q-A was over I made a call and got him a ride out on Bashti Levant's plane."

"I can't—" Charlotte broke off.

"You can't what."

Charlotte shrugged.

"You can't what, Charlotte."

"I can't see Warren on a small plane with Bashti Levant for five hours." She had just seized on this but it was true. Bashti Levant was in the music business. Bashti Levant had "labels," and three-piece suits and large yellow teeth and obscure Balkan proclivities. "They won't like each other."

"No. They won't. They will cordially dislike each other and they will entirely entertain each other. That's not what you were going to say. You can't what."

Charlotte gave up on the scarf. "I can't deal with Warren right now."

"What's to 'deal with'? You were married to him, now you're married to me. You think you're the only two people in the world who used to fuck and don't any more?"

"Not at all." Another thing Charlotte could not deal with was Leonard's essentially rational view of the sexual connection. "There's also you and me."

"Not bad. You're waking up." Leonard seemed pleased. "Here's a taxi."

"I think I'll walk."

"Then walk," Leonard said as he got into the taxi.

Charlotte walked as far as Grace Cathedral and stood for a while just inside the nave in a particular pool of yellow light Marin had liked as a child. When the light shifted on the window and there was no more yellow Charlotte left the cathedral. She intended walking back to the Fairmont to get a taxi but there was one idling outside the cathedral, and Leonard was waiting in it, just as he had been waiting in a taxi outside the courthouse the morning she divorced Warren.

"She had a straw hat one Easter." Charlotte had taken Leonard's hand in the taxi but neither of them spoke until the house on California Street was in sight. "And a flowered lawn dress."

"Don't think you have to get yourself pregnant just to prove he doesn't have you any more, Charlotte."

"We took her to lunch at the Carlyle, I remember she was cold."

"Don't make the mistake of thinking you can just run it back through the projector, Charlotte."

"Warren gave her his coat."

Upstairs in the house on California Street Charlotte took off her skirt and sweater and laid them on a chair. She took off the pieces of handmade navy-blue underwear and let them drop to the floor. At the bottom of a drawer she found a faded flannel nightgown and she pulled on the nightgown and she lay on the bed and watched the last light leave the windows.

"And we drank a lot of Ramos Fizzes. And in the middle of lunch Warren said he had an appointment downtown. And when the check came I didn't have any money. I didn't even have two dollars for a taxi, Marin and I walked home." She turned to Leonard. "She was three. Everybody admired her hat. I think I was never so happy on a Sunday. Why are you bringing him out?"

"He's her father, isn't he."

"I can't handle it."

Leonard sat on the edge of the bed and picked up the handmade pieces of navy-blue silk from the floor. They were very plain. They had no lace or embroidery. They had only the rows of infinitesimal stitches. "Maybe I want to see if you can. Somebody in the Azores went blind making these."

"Why do you have to bring him out."

"Because he gave her his coat," Leonard said.

"Somebody in the Philippines," Charlotte said. "Not the Azores. The Philippines."

8

"THOSE WERE FOUR TRULY WONDERFUL SPECIMENS you condemned me to fly out here with," Warren said when he walked into the house on California Street at nine-thirty the next morning.

Charlotte stood perfectly still. Warren looked as if he had not slept in several days. His eyes were bloodshot, his chin stubbled. He was wearing sneakers and a muffler Charlotte recognized as one she had knit for herself the winter they lived in an unheated apartment on East 93rd Street, and he was carrying not a suitcase but two shopping bags stuffed with what appeared to be dirty laundry. He was also carrying one red rose, which he handed to Charlotte without looking at her.

"Four authentic gargoyles," he said. "Some favor you did me. The four worst people in the world. Climbers. Vermin. Gargoyles. New York trash. Hogarth caricatures. 25,000 feet, no exit. Deliver me from favors. I need a drink."

"You repeated gargoyles," Leonard said. "Otherwise vintage."

"The FBI is due at ten," Charlotte said.

"What's that got to do with your getting me a drink. Me no get FBI joke."

"I haven't heard that since it was still 'me no get Indian joke,'" Leonard said. "Which I remember vividly from the night I introduced you to the Maharanee of wherever she was from."

"Lower Pelham," Warren said. "She was the Maharanee of Lower Pelham." He dropped the shopping bags on the floor in front of the fireplace. An aerosol can of shaving cream and a balled seersucker suit stuffed with dirty socks rolled out. "Get somebody to wash and iron that, Charlotte, all right? The suit just needs pressing."

"We don't have any washers and ironers on the place today." Charlotte retrieved the aerosol can before it hit the open fire. "Or any pressers."

"I can see you're in one of your interesting moods. Tell me what else you can't do for me today, Charlotte. You think you can give me a drink? Or can't you."

Charlotte filled a glass with ice and splashed bourbon into it. Her hands were shaking. The veins on her arms were standing out and she did not want Warren to see them. When she finally spoke her voice was neutral. "Who exactly was on this plane?"

"All friends of yours, I have no doubt. Which reminds me, you look like hell, your veins show." Warren took the glass and drained it. "This Levant creature, whoever he is."

"Bashti Levant controls three out of five pop records sold in America." Leonard seeemed amused. "As you know perfectly well."

"Yeah, well, I had some fun at his expense, I don't mind telling you. I had a little fun with him and this fat castrato he had along to bray at his jokes. This patsy Palm Beach castrato. 'P.L.U.,' he kept saying. 'People Like Us.' I let him know what category that was, don't think I didn't. Fawning capon. French cuffs. Parasitical eunuch."

"You didn't like him," Leonard said.

"Palm Beach trash hanger-on. I let the women alone."

"The last Southern gentleman," Leonard said.

"Not that they deserved it. Two terrible women. Terrible voices, terrible brays. The castrato only brayed when the Levant creature snapped his fingers, but the women brayed all the time. 3,000 miles of braying. *Le island. Le weekend. Les monkey-gland injections. Le* New York trash." Warren held out his glass to Charlotte. "I believe one of them was married to the Levant creature. Whoever he is, I have no idea."

"That surprises me. Since Leonard just told you."

"That surprises you, does it." Warren rattled the ice in his glass. "You surprise easier than you used to. I suppose this creature is a client of Leonard's."

"As a matter of fact he is."

"Leonard's got all the luck. Arabs. Jews. Indians. Bashti Levant."

"Niggers," Leonard said. "You forgot niggers."

"How exactly did this creature come to your attention, Leonard? He rape an Arab? Or is that possible. Actually I believe that's a solecism. Raping an Arab."

"You've had that Arab in the wings, I can tell by your delivery." Leonard took Warren's glass and filled it. "I got involved with Bashti on a dope charge a few years ago. Involving certain of his artists."

"I don't believe what I'm hearing. Bashti's artists."

"There was a civil-liberties issue."

"Of course there was." Warren choked with laughter and slapped his knee. "I knew there was."

92

"There was," Charlotte said.

In the silence that followed she could hear her voice echo, harsh and ugly. She fixed her eyes on the ring Leonard had brought her from wherever he had gone to meet the man who financed the Tupamaros.

The square emerald ring.

The big square emerald from some capital she could not remember.

"Listen to that voice," Warren said. "Let's have that tone of voice again."

Leonard looked at Charlotte and shook his head slightly.

Charlotte picked up a cigarette and lit it.

"No wonder your daughter left home," Warren said.

The red rose Warren had given Charlotte fell from the table to the floor.

Charlotte said nothing.

"All I hold against your daughter is she didn't catch Bashti Levant with that pipe bomb. Bashti and certain of his artists. That's the only bone I want to pick with your daughter. Your daughter and mine."

"He doesn't mellow," Leonard said finally.

"What did you expect, Leonard? You expect I'd hit forty-five and start applauding the family of man?" Warren drained his second drink. "It's my birthday, Charlotte. You haven't wished me happy birthday."

"I'll tell you something I expected, I expected—" Charlotte broke off. She did not know what she had expected. She concentrated on the emerald.

Bogotá.

Quito.

She had no idea where Leonard had met the man who financed the Tupamaros.

93

"Today's not your birthday," she said finally. "Your birthday was last month."

"Your husband expected a humanist."

"Leonard," Leonard said.

"Pardon?"

"Her husband's name is Leonard."

"I stole that rose for you," Warren said. "Off the flight of the living dead."

Dwelling on the past leads to unsoundness and dementia, my aunt also advised.

And, *Don't cry over curdled milk, Grace, make cottage cheese of it.*

And to the same doubtful point: *Remember Lot's Wife, avoid the backward glance.*

"Wish me happy birthday," Warren said. "Have a drink on my forty-fifth birthday."

"Your birthday was October 23rd," Charlotte said.

"She doesn't drink before breakfast," Leonard said. "It's hard and fast with her, she never does."

"She did on my thirtieth," Warren said.

"Which was on October 23rd nineteen-hundred and —oh shit."

"Watch your language," Warren said.

Avoid the backward glance.

Until Marin disappeared Charlotte had arranged her days to do exactly that.

94

9

I KNOW WHY CHARLOTTE LIKED TALKING TO THE
FBI: the agents would let her talk about Marin. Their
devotion to Marin seemed total. They were pilgrims
pledged to the collection of relics from Marin's passion.
During the days before Warren arrived in San Francisco the agents had taken Charlotte to see Marin's
apartment on Haste Street in Berkeley. The agents had
taken Charlotte to see the house on Grove Street in
Berkeley where they had found the cache of .30-caliber
Browning automatic rifles and the translucent pink
orthodontal retainer Marin was supposed to wear to
correct her bite. In both those places the gray morning
light fell through dusty windows onto worn hardwood
floors and Charlotte had remembered for the first time
how sad she herself had been at Berkeley before Warren came to her door.

"Let's flop back to one of the theories you were
espousing yesterday, Mrs. Douglas. When you—"

"Let's flop back to all of them," Warren said.
Warren had been sitting in the same chair ever since

he walked into the house and dropped his shopping bags. He had gotten up only to get himself drinks and once, perfunctorily, when the FBI men arrived and Leonard left. "I'm the felon's father," he had said to the FBI men. He seemed bent now in a fit of laughter. "I want to flop back to every one of these theories Mrs. Douglas has been espousing. In my absence. I've been out of touch, I didn't know Mrs. Douglas had theories. To espouse."

"When I what?" Charlotte said.

"Flip flop. We need ice, Charlotte."

"When you—" The FBI man glanced uneasily at Warren. "When you said yesterday that Marin 'might have been sad,' what exactly did you mean? Normal everyday blues? Or something more, uh, out of the mainstream?"

"Just your normal everyday mainstream power-to-the-people *latifundismo* Berkeley blues." Warren was still bent with laughter. "Just those old Amerikan blues. Spell that with a K."

"I don't know what I meant," Charlotte said.

"Some theory," Warren said. "Did you get the K? Did you spell it with a K?"

"To push on for a moment, Mrs. Douglas, the office raised one other question. Did your daughter ever mention a Russian, name of, uh, let's see."

The FBI man examined his notebook.

"Those old Amerikan blues didn't *come* up the river from New Orleans, they K-O-M-E up the river from New Orleans. Get it? Charlotte? Did he get the K?"

"He got it."

"Gurdjieff," the FBI man said. "Russian, name of Gurdjieff. Marin ever mention him?"

"In the first place he was an Armenian," Warren said. "Otherwise you're on top of the case."

"I'm not sure I get your meaning, Mr. Bogart."

"Not at all. You're doing fine."

"Excuse me. The Gurdjieff I'm thinking of is a Russian."

"Excuse me. The Gurdjieff you're thinking of is Bashti Levant."

"Warren. Please."

"Don't you think that's funny, Charlotte? 'Excuse me, the Gurdjieff you're thinking of is Bashti Levant'?"

"It's funny, Warren. Now—"

"You used to think I was funny."

"Let me try to put this on track." The FBI man cleared his throat. "Marin ever mention a Gurdjieff of *any* nationality? Ever mention reading about him?"

"No," Charlotte said.

"Marin can't read," Warren said. "She plays a good game of tennis, she's got a nice backhand, good strong hair and an IQ of about 103."

Charlotte closed her eyes.

"Charlotte. Face facts. Credit where credit is due, you raised her. She's boring."

"I'm not sure this is a productive tack," the FBI man said.

"Irving's not sure this is a productive tack." Warren rattled his ice. "Hear, hear, Charlotte. Listen to Irving."

"Bruno," the FBI man said. "The name is Bruno Furetta."

"Don't mind me, Irving, I've been drinking."

"I happen to know you're not all that drunk, Warren." Charlotte did not open her eyes. "I happen to know you're just amusing yourself. As usual."

"You get the picture."

Charlotte stood up. "And I want to tell you that *I am not*—"

"She's overwrought," Charlotte heard Warren say as she fled the room. "Let me give you some advice, Irving. Never mind the Armenians, *cherchez le tennis pro.*"

10

"Boo hoo," warren said when he came upstairs an hour later. "What happened to your sense of
humor?"

Charlotte said nothing. Very deliberately she closed
the book she had been trying to read since the day
after the FBI first came to the house on California
Street. The book was a detailed analysis of the three
rose windows at Chartres, not illustrated, and every
time Charlotte picked it up she began again on page
one. She did not want Warren in the room. She did
not want Warren to be in any room where she slept
with Leonard, did not want him to see Leonard's
Seconal and her hand cream together on the table by
the bed, did not want to see him examining the neck-
ties that Leonard had that morning tried, rejected, and
left on the bed. In fact she did not want him to see the
bed at all.

"We don't have anything in common any more."
Warren picked up a yellow silk tie and knotted it
around his collar. "You and me. Leonard won't miss

this, he's jaundiced enough. You ever noticed? He's got a bad color?"

"One thing we have in common is that we both agree that as far as having anything in common goes—" Charlotte broke off. She was watching a tube of KY jelly on the table by the bed. She did not see any way to move it into the drawer without attracting Warren's attention. "As far as having anything in common goes, we don't have anything. In common."

"You sound like you had a stroke. You had a stroke?"

"I happen to have a headache."

"You mean I happen to give you a headache."

"I mean I want you to leave this room."

"Don't worry, I'll leave this room." Warren sat on the bed, picked up the tube of KY jelly and put it in the drawer. "I don't like this room."

Charlotte said nothing.

"I only flew out here to see how you were."

Still Charlotte said nothing.

"I don't like your room, I don't like your house, I don't like your life." Warren picked up a silver box from the table by the bed. The box held marijuana and played "Puff the Magic Dragon" when the lid was lifted. Warren lifted the lid and looked at Charlotte. "I bet the two of you talk about 'turning on.' See what I mean about your life?"

"Go away," Charlotte whispered.

"Excuse me. I mean your 'life-style.' You don't have a life, you have a 'life-style.' You still look good, though."

"Go away."

Warren looked at her for a while before he spoke.

"I want you to come to New Orleans with me."

Charlotte tried to concentrate on meeting Leonard

100

for lunch. Very soon she would walk out of this room and down the stairs. She would walk out of this house and she would take a taxi to the Tadich Grill, alone.

"I said I want you to come to New Orleans with me, are you deaf? Or just rude."

She would go in the taxi alone to meet Leonard at the Tadich Grill.

"I want you to see Porter with me. Porter is dying. Porter wants to see you. Do this one thing for me."

Charlotte tried to keep her mind on whether to order sand dabs or oysters at the Tadich Grill. Porter was a distant cousin of Warren's. During the five years Charlotte and Warren were married Porter had invested $25,000 in an off-Broadway play that Warren never wrote, $30,000 in a political monthly that Warren never took beyond its dummy issue, and $2,653.84 in ransoming Warren's and her furniture and Marin's baby clothes from the Seven Santini Brothers Storage Company in Long Island City. Charlotte did not even like Porter.

Sand dabs.

No.

Oysters.

"If you won't do it for me you'll do it for Porter. Or you're a worse human being than even I think."

"I can't just leave. Can I."

"You're not leaving, you're paying a visit to Porter. Who is dying. Who loves you."

"I can't forgive Porter what he said to Leonard. At dinner out here. Two years ago. He behaved badly." In fact Charlotte could not even recall what Porter had said to Leonard, but whenever she talked to Warren she fell helplessly into both his diction and his rosary of other people's disloyalties. "I just can't forgive Porter that at all."

101

"Porter loves you."

"Leonard had to ask him to leave the house."

"What's that got to do with you."

There did not seem to Charlotte any ground on which this question could safely be met. She put it from her mind.

"I said what's that got to do with you."

Charlotte stood up, walked to the dressing room, and took a coat from the closet.

"Porter's dying, Charlotte."

Charlotte put the coat over her shoulders.

"Porter's dying and you're putting on your mink coat. You got Hadassah today? Mah-Jongg? You get the picture about your life?"

"It's not mink. It's sable. I have a lunch date."

"Say that again."

"I said: *I have a lunch date*. With Leonard."

"Don't let me keep you. Somebody who loves you is dying, your only child is lost, I'm asking you one last favor, and you've got a lunch date." Warren opened the lid of the silver box again. The mechanism began to play. "You getting it? You getting the picture? You're never going to see Marin again but never mind, you've got a lunch date? And maybe after your 'lunch date' you and your interesting husband can, what do you call it, 'get stoned'?"

"You *fuck*," Charlotte screamed.

Warren smiled.

Charlotte grabbed a pair of scissors and clutched them, point out.

Charlotte's sable coat fell to the floor.

"You walk into the house four hours ago, you haven't said Marin's *name* except to make fun of her. You try to use Marin on me, you don't give a *fuck* about—"

102

Warren still smiled.

The music box still played "Puff the Magic Dragon."

Charlotte looked at her hand and opened it and the scissors fell to the floor. "About Marin," she said.

"Time and fevers," Warren said finally. His voice was tired. "Burn away."

"I don't know what you're saying."

"I'm not saying, babe. I'm quoting. 'And the grave proves the child ephemeral.' Who am I quoting?"

"Shakespeare. Milton. I don't know who you're quoting. Make that thing stop playing."

"Auden. W. H. Auden. You aren't any better read than you ever were, I'll give you that." Warren closed the box and picked up Charlotte's coat from the floor. "'But in my arms till break of day let the living creature lie.' Where's your lunch?"

"I can't go to lunch." She stood like a child and let Warren put the coat on her shoulders. "I can't go to lunch crying."

"Where was your lunch?"

"Tadich's."

"Sure," Warren said. "Let's eat some fish."

Warren entertained Leonard at lunch with news of an automotive heir they both knew who was devoting his fortune to Micronesian independence; excused himself five times to make telephone calls; canceled the oysters Leonard had ordered for Charlotte because Pacific oysters would not compare with Gulf oysters; ordered oysters himself, drank three gin martinis and a German beer, fed Charlotte with his own fork because she was too thin not to eat, left the restaurant before Leonard ordered coffee and did not reappear that afternoon or evening. In the morning Charlotte told Leonard that she could not stay in the same house with

Warren. Leonard moved Warren to a motel in the Marina, and paid for the room a week in advance. Charlotte stayed upstairs until they were gone. I understand what Warren Bogart could do to Charlotte Douglas because I met him, later, once in New Orleans: he had the look of a man who could drive a woman like Charlotte right off her head.

I have no idea what I meant by "a woman like Charlotte."

I suppose I mean only a woman so convinced of the danger that lies in the backward glance.

I might have said a woman so unstable, but I told you, Charlotte performed the tracheotomy, Charlotte dropped the clinic apron at the colonel's feet. I am less and less convinced that the word "unstable" has any useful meaning except insofar as it describes a chemical compound.

11

IN THE SECOND WEEK AFTER THE RELEASE OF Marin's tape Leonard flew to Montreal to meet with leaders of a Greek liberation movement. A man who described himself as a disillusioned Scientologist called Charlotte to say that Marin was under the influence of a Clear in Shasta Lake. A masseuse at Elizabeth Arden called Charlotte to say that she had received definite word from Edgar Cayce via Mass Mind that Marin was with the Hunzas in the Himalayas. The partially decomposed body of a young woman was found in a shallow grave on the Bonneville Salt Flats but the young woman's dental work differed conclusively from Marin's.

Charlotte watched the rain blowing across California Street.

Leonard flew from Montreal to Chicago to speak at a Days of Rage memorial.

"You want to see bad teeth, get on down here," Warren said to Charlotte the first night he telephoned. He was calling not from the motel in the Marina but from the Polo Lounge of the Beverly Hills Hotel, where he had flown with Bashti Levant and one of his English bands. "The algae on the genetic pool. They drink Mai Tais. Get it?"

"I don't understand what you're doing there."

"I'm not screwing their women, if that's what you think. Not even with yours, Basil. 'Basil.' 'Ian.' 'Andrew.' English Jews. You over your homicidal mood?"

Charlotte said nothing.

"The women all had lobotomies at fourteen, but the teeth stop me. Will you see Porter on his deathbed or won't you?"

"What exactly is Porter dying of."

"Porter is dying of that long disease his life. Alexander Pope, lost on you. Never mind what Porter's dying of. Do it for me."

"I don't even believe Porter's dying. If Porter were dying I wouldn't think you'd be hanging around the Beverly Hills Hotel. With people you say you can't stand."

"I'm not 'hanging around,' Charlotte, I'm 'hanging out.' The phrase is 'hanging out.' You always did have a tin ear. Will you come to New Orleans or won't you."

"I won't."

"Why won't you?"

"Because if I went to New Orleans with you," Charlotte said, "I would end up murdering you. I would take a knife and murder you. In your sleep."

"I don't sleep anyway."

Charlotte said nothing.

"It doesn't matter to me what you do. Go, don't go. Come, don't come. Murder me, don't murder me. I'm only telling you what you have to do for your own peace of mind."

"I have had that shit," Charlotte whispered, and hung up.

"I would bet my life on your having some character," Warren said the second night he telephoned from the Beverly Hills Hotel. "Lucky for me I didn't."

Charlotte said nothing.

"Not that it matters. Not that it's worth anything. My life."

Charlotte said nothing.

"You're going to remember this, Charlotte. I tried to tell you what to do. You're going to lie awake and remember this for the rest of your miserable unfortunate life."

Charlotte said nothing.

Charlotte believed that there was something familiar about this telephone call but for a moment she could not put her finger on what it was. There had been something else she was supposed to lie awake and remember for the rest of her miserable unfortunate life.

Leaving him.

That was it.

She tried to put that other telephone call back out of her mind. It must have been after she left him, the other telephone call, because she had never exactly told him that she was leaving him. She had told him that she was going to her mother's funeral. This was true but not the whole truth. Her mother had just died and she was going to have some money to take care of herself and Marin and she did not want to give the money to Warren and she took Marin and flew out of Idlewild and never went back.

"You hear me, Charlotte?"

She had cried all the way to San Francisco and Marin had been asleep on her lap and she remembered the landing and Marin's pale hair damp and sticky with sleep and tears.

"Charlotte? They ever mention sins of omission in those wonderful Okie schools you went to?"

For the rest of that week when the telephone rang between one and four A.M. Charlotte would hang up as soon as she heard Warren's voice. A few days later a copy of *Time* arrived with a photograph that showed Charlotte leaving the house on California Street with her hands over her face, and Charlotte wrote a letter to the editor pointing out that the description of her as a "reclusive socialite" was a contradiction in terms. Leonard returned from Chicago and asked Charlotte not to mail the letter.

"I just remembered I never told Warren I was leaving him," Charlotte said to Leonard.

"He's had fifteen years, I guess he's figured it out," Leonard said to Charlotte.

"I mean I just kissed him goodbye at Idlewild and said I'd be back in a week and I knew I wouldn't be."

"I know it."

"How could you know it."

"Because that's how you'll leave me."

"Fourteen years," Charlotte said. "Not fifteen. Fourteen."

Warren returned from Los Angeles and Leonard asked him to dinner but Warren did not arrive until eleven-thirty, accompanied by a 268-pound widow from Fort Worth he had met at Golden Gate Fields, the jockey who had that day ridden the woman's three-year-old filly to defeat, and a shy girl with long legs who was introduced to Leonard by Warren as the most brilliant mathematician at UCLA. Warren had met the most brilliant mathematician at UCLA at the pool of the Beverly Hills Hotel and had driven her Porsche north by way of Big Sur. She drank large quantities of apple juice and told Leonard that Marin could be located by sensitive programming of a Honeywell 782 solid-state computer. Charlotte had gone to bed with the book about the rose windows at Chartres and did not come downstairs. Charlotte had once taken Marin to see the glass at Chartres and Marin had cried because it was too beautiful.

Or so Charlotte said once.

Another time she told me that she herself had cried.

Still another time she told me that a British television crew had been filming inside the cathedral and she and Marin had been unable to see the glass at all because of the television lights.

I am now incapable of thinking about the glass at Chartres without seeing through every window the lights at the Tivoli Gardens.

12

"*I've never been afraid of the dark.*"

"*Actually I'm never depressed. Actually I don't believe in being depressed.*"

"*By the way. Marin and I are inseparable.*"

Accept those as statements of how Charlotte wished it had been.

Charlotte also told me once that she and Warren Bogart were "inseparable."

Charlotte also told me once that she and Leonard Douglas were "inseparable."

Charlotte even told me once that she and her brother Dickie were "inseparable," and adduced as evidence the fact that he had once given her a Christmas present no one else would have thought to give her: twenty-eight acres in southern Nevada.

Of course it had not been exactly that way at all.

Of course there had been the usual days and weeks and even months when Charlotte had been separated from everyone she knew by a grayness so dense that the brightness of even her own child in the house was

110

galling, insupportable, a reproach to be avoided at breakfast and on the stairs. During such periods Charlotte endured the usual intimations of erratic cell multiplication, dust and dry wind, sexual dysaesthesia, sloth, flatulence, root canal. During such periods Charlotte would rehearse cheerful dialogues she might need to have with Marin. For days at a time her answers to Marin's questions would therefore strike the child as weird and unsettling, cheerful but not quite responsive. "Do you think I'll get braces in fourth grade," Marin would ask. "You're going to love fourth grade," Charlotte would answer. During such periods Charlotte suffered the usual dread when forced to visit Marin's school and hear the doomed children celebrate all things bright and beautiful, all creatures great and small.

She would shut her ears.

She would watch Marin numbly, from the usual great distance.

She would hang on by the usual routines, fill in whole days by the usual numbers.

The problem was that Charlotte did not know that any of this was "usual."

Charlotte had no idea that anyone else had ever been afflicted by what she called the "separateness."

And because she did not she fought it, she denied it, she tried to forget it, and, during those first several weeks after Marin disappeared and obliterated all the numbers, spent many days without getting out of bed. I think I have never known anyone who led quite so unexamined a life.

13

CHARLOTTE DID NOT GET OUT OF BED THE DAY after she went with Pete Wright to open the safe-deposit box.

"I'm not sure your daughter appreciates the legal bind she's put you in, Char."

Pete Wright was examining some stock certificates. Charlotte had known Pete Wright longer than she had known Leonard, he had roomed at Stanford with Dickie and he had handled her divorce from Warren and as Leonard's junior partner he had paid a Christmas call every year with a suitable present for Marin, but there in the safe-deposit vault of the Wells-Fargo Bank on Powell Street he had kept referring to Marin as "your daughter." Charlotte did not want to hear about the legal bind she was in and she did not want Pete Wright to call her Char. Only Dickie called her Char. There was something else about Pete Wright that bothered her but she did not want to think about that either.

"You're in a bit of a pickle here, Char."

112

"That's exactly what you said when I left Warren. And you took this enormous legal problem to Leonard and Leonard said I wasn't."

Charlotte took a gold pin of her grandmother's from the safe-deposit box.

Charlotte imagined the gold pin attached to the firing pin of a bomb.

Pete Wright had come to New York once when she was married to Warren.

"And I wasn't."

"You weren't what."

"I wasn't in a bit of a pickle."

"I have nothing but respect for Leonard as a lawyer, Charlotte, but as you know, Leonard leaves the estate work to me." Pete Wright took a deep breath. "Now. What we have here are stock certificates worth X dollars a quarter in dividends—"

"Eight-hundred and seven. $807 a quarter. I looked it up when you called me."

"What I'm saying, Charlotte, is that these particular certificates are in your and your daughter's names as joint tenants. Her signature—"

"I can forge it, can't I."

"Not legally, no."

"All right. I won't cash the checks. It's $807 a quarter, it's nothing."

The gold pin had a broken clasp. As Charlotte held the pin in her fingers she had an abrupt physical sense of eating chicken à la king and overdone biscuits at her grandmother's house in Hollister.

Pete Wright.

Pete Wright had been in New York once and had taken her to the Palm for dinner.

"What may seem 'nothing' to you, Charlotte—"

"I suppose you're about to tell me that $807 a

quarter is the average annual income for a grape picker. Is that what you're about to tell me?"

"I'm about to overlook your hostility."

"Leonard leaves the estate work to you, you leave the grape pickers to Leonard. Is that fair?"

"We used to be friends, Charlotte, and I like to think—"

She could taste the soft bits of pimento in the chicken à la king.

She could smell the biscuits burning in the oven.

She could also smell citronella, and calamine lotion, and the sweetened milky emulsion in prescription bottles that contained aureomycin. She could taste the acrid goat cheese her father used to get from the man who ran his cattle on the ranch. Her father had died. She could feel crushed and browning in her hand the camellias her mother used to braid into her hair for birthday parties. Her mother had died. She had erased burned biscuits and citronella when Warren came to her door in Berkeley, and she seemed to have been busy since, but there in the safe-deposit vault of the Wells-Fargo Bank on Powell Street she was not so busy.

She had erased some other things too.

She had been too busy.

Charlotte closed her hand around the pin with the broken clasp and tried not to think how it could be attached to the firing pin of a bomb.

She had gotten drunk at the Palm with Pete Wright.

"I gather by your silence you think Warren might oppose it."

"Oppose what," Charlotte said.

"Oppose declaring your daughter legally dead."

Charlotte looked at Pete Wright.

"It's a legality. It doesn't mean anything, but it

would enable you to cash these particular dividend checks. Or sell this particular stock. Or whatever."

Charlotte picked up the certificates.

"As well as clarify the question of the ranch. Which I feel impelled to remind you is tied up in trust for her. A loose trust, granted, but——"

Charlotte tore the certificates in half.

Pete Wright gazed at the wall behind Charlotte and made a sucking noise with his teeth. "Warren's quite disturbed, I don't know if you realize that. He comes by the house, he drinks too much, he jumps all over Clarice about her hatha yoga class, he acts like——"

Her mother had died.

Warren had not come home the night she got drunk at the Palm with Pete Wright.

"You don't need to tell me what Warren acts like."

"I gather you and Warren have had some misunderstanding, the rights and wrongs of which are outside my purview, but——"

Her father had died.

Warren had called at four A.M. the night she got drunk at the Palm with Pete Wright and she had told him not to come home.

"——I must say I don't think you're solving anything by pretending there aren't certain complications to——"

People did die. People were loose in the world and left it, and she had been too busy to notice.

The morning after she got drunk at the Palm she and Warren had taken Marin to lunch at the Carlyle. Marin was cold.

"I'm trying to talk to you like a Dutch uncle," Pete Wright said.

Warren gave her his coat.

"I think I fucked you one Easter," Charlotte said.

For the next several days Charlotte wanted only to

eat the food she had eaten in Hollister but she had lost the recipes her mother had written out and Charlotte did not know the number of any couple who would come to the house on California Street and do chicken à la king and burned biscuits. When I think of Charlotte Douglas apprehending death at the age of thirty-nine in the safe-deposit vault of a bank in San Francisco it occurs to me that there was some advantage in having a mother who died when I was eight, a father who died when I was ten, before I was busy.

14

CHARLOTTE DID NOT GET OUT OF BED THE DAY after she met the woman named Enid Schrader.

"Mark spoke so very highly of you," the woman had said on the telephone. There had been in Enid Schrader's voice something Charlotte did not want to recognize: a forced gaiety, a haggard sprightliness, a separateness not unlike her own. "Of you and your beautiful home."

Mark Schrader was said to have been on the L–1011 with Marin. Mark Schrader had on his face, in the pictures Charlotte had seen of him, a pronounced scar from a harelip operation. It did not seem plausible to Charlotte that she could have met a boy with such a scar and forgotten him, nor did it seem plausible that anyone on the L–1011 with Marin had ever spoken highly of the house on California Street, but maybe the boy's mother was trying to tell her something. Maybe there was a code in that peculiar stilted diction. Maybe Enid Schrader knew where Marin was.

"I think we should meet," Charlotte said guardedly.

"Could you have lunch at all? Today? The St. Francis Grill?"

"Delightful. Why."

"Why what?"

"Why the St. Francis Grill?"

"I just thought—" Charlotte did not know what she had just thought. She had rejected the house because it was watched. She had hit upon the St. Francis Grill as a place where all corners of the room could be seen. "Is there somewhere you'd rather go?"

"Not at all, I don't keep up with where the beautiful people eat. Not to worry about my recognizing you, I've seen pictures of you."

"I've seen pictures of you too."

"Before," the woman said. "I meant before. Pictures of you and your beautiful home."

Charlotte had met the woman at one-thirty and at two-thirty the code remained impenetrable. The woman did not seem interested in talking about her son, or about Marin. The woman seemed interested instead in talking about a friend who had a decorator's card.

"You'll adore Ruthie." The woman was drinking daiquiris and had refused lunch. "I'm getting you together soonest, that's definite, a promise. Meanwhile I'll borrow her card and we'll do the trade-only places. How's Tuesday?"

"How's Tuesday for what?" Charlotte said faintly.

"Monday's a no-no for me but if Tuesday's bad for you, let's say Wednesday. Earliest. Grab lunch where we find it."

"Listen." Charlotte glanced around the room before she spoke. "If there's something to see I think we should—I mean could we see it now?"

"But I haven't got Ruthie's card. I mean unless *you*

have a card—" The woman looked up. "What's the matter?"

"I don't think I know what you're talking about."

"I'm talking about taking you shopping." The woman's eyes reddened and filled with tears. "Unless of course you're too busy. But of course you are. Too busy."

Charlotte touched the woman's hand.

The last woman Charlotte had known to talk about "shopping" was her mother.

The last time Charlotte had been asked to go "shopping" it had been by her mother.

"Your ex-husband isn't too busy. I heard him on the radio. He was blotto but he talked to me. I called in to chat, he wasn't too busy to chat. Although blotto. On the radio. Whatever his name is."

"Warren." Charlotte did not want to hear about Warren on the radio. Leonard had once said that Warren could arrive in a town where he knew no one and within twenty-four hours he would have had dinner at the country club, been offered a temporary chair in Southern politics at the nearest college, and been on the radio. Charlotte did not want to think about Warren on the radio and she did not want to think why Enid Schrader was crying and she did not want to think about her mother shopping. Her mother had been shopping the day she died, at Ransohoff's. "His name is Warren Bogart."

"Whatever. The little whore's father."

The woman gave one last cathartic sob.

Charlotte reached for the check.

"My treat," the woman cried, her voice again sprightly. "You do it next time."

All the next day Charlotte could not erase from her mind the first newspaper picture she had seen of Enid

Schrader's son. "They'll ditch the harelip," Leonard had said when she showed him the picture. "The harelip's the fresh meat they'll throw on the trail, they can't afford him, Marin's not stupid."

"I wouldn't rely on that," Warren had said.

Another picture Charlotte could not erase from her mind was her mother alone at Ransohoff's.

I knew my mother was dead when I saw them carry out her bed to be burned, my father could not tell me. I knew my father was dead when the doorman at the Brown Palace would not let me go upstairs, he sent for a maid to tell me. She brought an éclair and cocoa. I waited for her on a red plush banquette. Unlike Charlotte I learned early to keep death in my line of sight, keep it under surveillance, keep it on cleared ground and away from any brush where it might coil unnoticed. The morning Edgar died I called Victor, signed the papers, walked out to Progreso as usual and ate lunch on the sea wall.

15

"I HAVE A LOUSY TRIP TO PHILADELPHIA, LOUSY flight back, I watch my own plane blow a tire on closed-circuit TV, I go to my office, I find Suzy in tears because Warren's camped in her one-room apartment, I come home and I find my wife hasn't gotten *dressed* in two days. I finish this call, Charlotte, I'm going to trot your ass over to Polly Orben's office, this isn't healthy." Leonard uncupped the receiver and spoke into it. "Try the other line, Suzy, see if you can keep your finger off the disconnect this time."

"Why don't you trot Suzy's ass over to Polly Orben's office," Charlotte said without turning around. She was watching the FBI man in the window of the apartment across the street. "Why don't you trot Warren's ass over to Polly Orben's office."

"Tell him we're going to trade off the felony and plead the two misdemeanors," Leonard said into the telephone.

"*Warren* and Polly Orben would be good," Charlotte said.

121

"And tell him I don't want any of that boom-boom shit at the hearing." Leonard hung up the telephone. "Speaking of Warren he says you won't see him. He says you misunderstand him."

"The *fuck* I misunderstand him."

"Felicitously put," Leonard said after a while. "In any case I told him to come by."

"Tell him I'm in Hollister. Tell him I'm in Hollister and about how there's no telephone on the ranch."

"There are eight telephones on the ranch. On three separate lines."

"He doesn't know that."

"For Christ's sake, Charlotte, *go* to Hollister if you don't want to see him. Go now. Go right now."

"I can't actually go to Hollister."

"Why can't you, besides the fact that it might entail getting dressed."

She could not go to Hollister because she was afraid Warren might find her there, alone at the ranch. She could not go to Hollister because if Warren found her there alone at the ranch something bad would happen. This seemed so obvious to Charlotte that she could not bring herself to say it. "I can't go to Hollister because you have people coming to the house for lunch tomorrow."

"Tell me who I have coming to the house for lunch tomorrow."

"Coming to the house for lunch tomorrow you have . . ." She could not think.

"Coming to the house for lunch tomorrow I have . . . the leaders of . . . two dissident factions within . . . the Haight-Divisadero Coalition. You got a whole lot you want to say to them?"

Charlotte picked up a brush and began attacking her hair in abrupt chops.

"On the subject of day-care versus guerrilla theater? Maybe we could get Dickie and Linda up from Hollister and get their thinking?"

"I don't know why you put all those telephones on the ranch anyway."

"I don't know, Charlotte. Communication?"

"Nobody in my family ever found it necessary to keep three different calls going on that ranch."

"Nobody in your family ever found it necessary to pay the taxes on that ranch, either. Tell me again why you can't go to Hollister."

The hair Charlotte pulled from her brush was dry and wiry and faded.

When Marin was small she had played a game with Charlotte's hair and called it gold.

"I feel so old," Charlotte said.

"Tell me why you can't go to Hollister."

"I keep remembering things."

"Most of us do. Tell me why you won't see Warren."

"You don't know what he wants."

"Of course I know what he wants. He wants you back. You think I make my living being dense?"

"Then *why did you ask?*"

Leonard lifted a mass of Charlotte's hair and let it drop through his fingers. "Because I was interested in whether you knew it. You don't look so old."

16

WHO CAN SAY WHY I CRAVE THE LIGHT IN BOCA
Grande, who can say why my body grows cancers.

Who can say why Charlotte left Leonard Douglas.

Maybe she thought it was easier.

Maybe she believed herself loose in the world, maybe
she was tired, maybe she had just remembered that
people died. Maybe she thought that if she walked
back into the Carlyle Hotel on Easter morning with
Warren Bogart Marin would be there, in a flowered
lawn dress.

"It's too late," she said to her gynecologist the
morning he confirmed that she was carrying Leonard's
child. "It didn't happen in time."

Somebody cuts you.

Where it doesn't show.

I have no way of knowing about the cuts that don't
show.

I know only that during the fifth week after the
release of Marin's tape Charlotte woke early every
morning, dressed promptly, and immersed herself in

the domestic maintenance of the house on California Street. She made inventories. She replaced worn sheets, chipped wine glasses, crazed plates. She paid an electrician time-and-a-half to rewire, on a Saturday, two crossed spots on the Jackson Pollock in the dining room. She was obsessed by errands, and she laid it to her pregnancy.

Leonard did not.

So entirely underwater did Charlotte live her life that she did not recognize her preoccupations as those of a woman about to abandon a temporary rental.

Leonard did.　　　—

17

PHOTOGRAPHS OF THE LAST EVENING CHARLOTTE spent with Leonard Douglas appeared a year later in *Vogue,* Charlotte showed them to me.

There was Leonard, standing with an actor at the party in Beverly Hills, standing with his head bent, listening to the actor but looking somewhere else.

There was Charlotte, sitting with an actress at the party in Beverly Hills, Charlotte smiling, her eyes wide and glazed and in the end as impenetrable as Marin's.

She had not meant to go with Leonard to the party in Beverly Hills at all.

She had not even meant to go with Leonard to the airport.

But on the fifth day of the fifth week after the release of Marin's tape she had opened the door of the house on California Street and found Warren standing there.

"I guess you can give me a drink."

"Actually I'm just about to drive Leonard to the airport." She followed his gaze to the limousine idling at the curb. She had not, until that moment, intended going to the airport. "I mean I'm not exactly driving him to the airport but I'm driving *with* him to the airport."

"I guess there's room for me."

"Actually you don't want to drive to the airport, it could take hours." She had not in fact spoken to Warren since the nights he called from the Beverly Hills Hotel on Bashti Levant's bill. "This time of day. The traffic."

"I've got time."

"Hours. Literally."

"You're swimming upstream, Charlotte."

In the car Charlotte had sat on the jump seat and fixed her eyes on the driver's pigtail.

"While you were upstairs Warren was telling me about this ninety-two-year-old Trotskyist he drinks with in New York," Leonard said. "This Trotskyist lives at the Hotel Albert. Naturally."

"Charlotte knows Benny," Warren said. "You remember Benny, Charlotte."

Charlotte had not remembered Benny. Charlotte had not even thought that she was meant to remember Benny, whoever Benny was. Benny was only Warren's way of reminding her that he had a prior claim.

"This Trotskyist drinks Pisco Sours," Leonard said.

"Sazeracs," Warren said. "Not Pisco Sours. Sazeracs. Benny always asks about you, Charlotte. You ought to go see him, he's not going to live forever."

Charlotte kept her eyes on the driver's pigtail.

"Neither is Porter," Warren said. "In case you forgot."

"Neither is Charlotte," Leonard said. "You keep this up. Something I've never been able to understand is how you happen to know more Trotskyists than Trotsky did."

"You know more Arabs, it evens out. What am I going to tell Porter, Charlotte?"

"All of them ninety-two years old," Leonard said.

"I said what am I going to tell Porter, Charlotte."

"All of them sitting around the Hotel Albert drinking Pisco Sours," Leonard said.

"Sazeracs. What do you want me to tell Porter on his deathbed, Charlotte."

"Personally I want you to tell Porter about this ninety-two-year-old Trotskyist," Leonard said. "You're overplaying your hand, Warren. You're pushing her too hard while she's still got an ace. I'll lay you odds, she's going to see her ace. She's going to say she's coming with me."

"But I am." Charlotte looked at Leonard for the first time. "I am definitely coming with you. I always was."

"No," Leonard said. "You were not 'always' coming with me. You see, Warren? Bad hand. You didn't pace your play."

"But I always wanted to go with you," Charlotte said.

"Definitely you always wanted to go with him," Warren said. "You haven't met enough Arabs."

"He's going to Los Angeles and Miami," Charlotte said.

"Or enough Jews," Warren said.

Because Charlotte had gotten on the plane with no bag and because Leonard's presence was required at the party where the photographs were taken, a $250-a-ticket benefit in a tent behind someone's house in Beverly Hills, Charlotte was wearing, at the time she was photographed, a dress borrowed from the wife of the record executive who had organized the evening, a dress made entirely of colored ribbons.

"You shouldn't have told Warren to keep the car," she had said as she put on the dress. "He'll keep it all night. I look absurd."

"You wouldn't if you had a tambourine," Leonard said. "He'll keep it all week."

Charlotte sat down. She was very tired. She did not think she had ever been so tired. She did not see how she could finish tying the ribbons on the dress.

"Sometimes I wish," Leonard said after a while. He began tying the ribbons Charlotte had abandoned. "I don't know."

"Sometimes you wish what."

"Sometimes I wish you could just fuck him and get it over with."

"I don't want to."

"Charlotte. Shit. I know you don't *want* to."

A stage had been constructed over the swimming pool of the house in Beverly Hills and several entertainers auctioned their services, singing and dancing and placing surprise telephone calls to friends and relatives of high bidders. Leonard raised five hundred dollars by dancing the limbo under a pole held by the record executive's wife, a young woman with pale blond hair like Marin's and a Brahmin caste mark painted on her forehead, and, at Charlotte's table, an actress who had visited Hanoi spoke of the superior health and beauty of the children there.

"It's because they aren't raised by their mothers," the actress said. "They don't have any of that bourgeois personal crap laid on them."

Charlotte studied her wine glass and tried to think

129

of something neutral to say to the actress. She wanted to get up but her chair was blocked by three men who seemed to be discussing the financing of a motion picture, or a war.

"No mama-papa-baby-nuclear-family bullshit," the actress said. "It's beautiful."

Charlotte concentrated on the details of the financing, the part to be played by the Canadians, the controls exerted by the Crédit Suisse.

"I know why you're crying," the actress said after a while.

Morocco would lend its army. Spain would not. Two-eight above the line.

"And I'm sorry, but that's exactly the kind of personal crap I never saw in Hanoi."

The flash bulb blazed.

Charlotte smiled.

The flash bulb dropped on the table.

"Did you know I spent a night once with Pete Wright," Charlotte said to Leonard as he led her from the table. "Did you know I did that and forgot it."

"You didn't forget it at all," Leonard said. "You told me the first night I met you."

"I am so tired. I am so tired of remembering things. Leonard. Tell me it's because I'm pregnant."

"I wish I could," Leonard said.

Leonard took Charlotte back to the Beverly Wilshire but she continued crying so Leonard, because he was due in Miami the next day to assist in the sale of four French Mirages from one Caribbean independency to another, called the record executive and borrowed a company Lear to fly Charlotte home. $216,000 was raised that night to benefit some one of Leonard's clients, Charlotte was unsure which until she saw the pictures in *Vogue*. She left the dress made entirely of colored ribbons on the floor of the suite at the Beverly Wilshire. I look at those pictures now and I see only Charlotte's smile.

18

"It's Charlotte," she said to her brother's wife from a pay phone on the highway outside Hollister. "I wondered if you and Dickie were going to be home."

"Richard and I play tennis every Saturday." There was a pause. "You want to use the pool, come on by, of course the heater's off."

"I thought I might see the children."

"They're at the gym."

There was a silence.

"Why exactly would I drive to Hollister to use your pool, Linda? I mean I get off a plane from Los Angeles and I sit in the airport all night and I rent a car and I'm out here on the highway and it's raining?"

Linda said nothing.

"Listen," Charlotte said finally. "Linda. Please ask me to dinner."

Before and during dinner Charlotte's brother drank steadily and did not mention Marin or Leonard or Warren. Linda sat at the table but refused to eat. She

132

said that she had eaten macaroni and cheese with the children, who seemed to have come home from and returned to the gym before Charlotte's arrival.

"They're just wonderful normal kids," Linda said after dinner. "Aren't they, Richard. No matter what Warren says."

"What's Warren got to do with it," Charlotte said.

"How would I know whether they're wonderful normal kids." Dickie opened another bottle of bourbon. "Maybe Warren's right, maybe they're boring, how would I know. They're always at the goddamn gym."

"Most people would consider that a definite plus. I believe your sister needs an ashtray."

"What's Warren got to do with it," Charlotte repeated.

"Or eating goddamn Kraft Dinners with you at four o'clock."

"Richard and I don't smoke," Linda said.

"We don't fuck either," Dickie said.

Charlotte put out her cigarette in an empty nut dish.

"Warren paid us a little visit," Linda said. "Lasting eleven hours and a quart and a half of gin."

"Charlotte's not interested in that, Linda."

"Tanqueray gin."

"Linda. We enjoyed seeing him, Char."

"He had this very interesting friend with him. He'd just run into this friend, they hadn't seen each other since the Roosevelt Hotel in New Orleans. Where—"

"I'm warning you, Linda."

"Where this friend of Warren's tended bar. Which is what this friend still does, except at the Pacific Union Club."

"I warned you, Linda. If Charlotte's husband wants

to bring a Negro to this house, this house is open. With bells on. All systems go."

"Charlotte's not married to Warren any more, Richard, you don't have to pretend you like him."

"Goddammit Linda, he's better than the Jew, isn't he?"

Linda began plumping pillows.

Dickie avoided Charlotte's eyes.

"Actually Leonard's not a Jew," Charlotte said. "Actually it just amuses Warren to say that Leonard's a Jew. A private joke. If you follow."

"Warren's sense of humor is just a little bit twisted," Linda said. "If you ask me."

"I didn't mean that about Leonard, Char. Hey. Char. I think Leonard is—"

"Not that anybody ever does ask me," Linda said.

"—A very fine lawyer," Dickie said.

"Listen," Charlotte said finally. Linda was still plumping pillows with pointed energy. "Dickie. I've been remembering some things since Marin left."

"That's no good for you, Char, remembering. Remembering is shit. Forget her."

"I'm not talking about Marin, I'm talking about—"

"Forget goddamn Marin. Forget goddamn Warren. You did your best. Forget the other one too."

"He doesn't want to talk about Marin, Charlotte." Linda turned off a lamp. "He wants to believe your life is just pluperfect."

"You turn off another plu-fucking-perfect light, Linda, I'm walking out of here with Charlotte and don't wait up."

"Lucky Charlotte."

"I'm not talking about Marin," Charlotte said. "I'm talking about when we lived on the ranch."

"Don't sell the ranch, Char."

"I'm not. I'm not talking about—do you remember how Nana would always burn the biscuits?"

"The ranch is the only home you've got, Char."

"Oh fine," Linda said. "Back to Tara. The Haveneyers are off to the races now. If you're looking for our car keys they're on the coffee table. Next to the ing from Massa Richard's glass."

"Remember the biscuits, Dickie? Halfway through dinner we'd smell them burning?"

"The only thing I remember your famous grandmother burning is every bedjacket I ever took her in the nursing home." Linda handed Charlotte her car keys. "Smoking in bed. Little holes in every one."

"You can't have forgotten the biscuits, Dickie."

"No good remembering, Char."

"Of course your sister wasn't here during that ordeal."

"Dickie," Charlotte said. "We used to laugh about it."

"You and me, Char." Dickie touched Charlotte's hair uncertainly and turned away. "Forget goddamn Marin. I say give her a Kraft Dinner and I say the hell with her."

Charlotte stayed that night in a motel off 101.

She tried to think about the biscuits but they kept fading out. She tried to think about the gold pin with the broken clasp but she kept seeing it on the bomb.

Her grandmother was dead and Marin was gone.

She had never gone shopping with her mother, she had never seen her father on Demerol, the ranch had eight telephones on three lines and Marin was gone.

It was Pete Wright who had told her that her father needed Demerol before he died.

The night she got drunk at the Palm.

She tried to think about Pete Wright in her bed that night but could not. She tried to think about Leonard in the bed of the house on California Street but she could see that bed only as it had been the day she picked up the scissors against Warren. She could see Warren sitting on that bed and she could also see Warren standing in front of her bed in New York the Easter morning after she got drunk at the Palm.

"Look at the slut on Easter morning."

She had screamed.

Marin had screamed.

She had picked up Marin and when Warren hit her again his hand glanced off Marin's temple.

She had picked up the kitchen knife.

She had thrown up.

She and Warren had taken Marin to the Carlyle and she had not had enough money to pay the bill. The beautiful *principessa*, the headwaiter had crooned over Marin. The beautiful *principessa,* the beautiful family. King of Crazy, Queen of Wrong. The headwaiter did not know that. The headwaiter would see to it that the bill was mailed. Charlotte lay on the motel bed and she thought about the beautiful *principessa* and about the beautiful family and about all the bills that had been mailed and never paid. She thought about all the unpaid bills and she thought about all the days and nights when she had promised Warren she would never leave.

There was another unpaid bill.

"You can't drink," Warren had said that Easter morning and held her shoulders as she threw up. "You can't drink at all, you never could." And then he washed her face and he took her to the Carlyle and she did not have enough money to pay the bill. Look at the slut on Easter morning. Marin had a straw hat one Easter, and a flowered lawn dress. Warren gave her his coat.

19

When Warren came that day to the door of the house on California Street Charlotte did not answer.

When Warren telephoned Charlotte hung up.

When Warren stood on the sidewalk outside the house on California Street at two A.M. and threw stones at the windows Charlotte closed the shutters.

When Warren left the note reading "THIS IS THE WORST BEHAVIOR YET" in the mailbox of the house on California Street Charlotte tore the note in half and avoided those rooms which fronted on the street.

When the two FBI men came to tell Charlotte that the boy with the harelip scar had been apprehended on an unrelated charge in Nogales, Arizona, and had hanged himself in his cell Charlotte left the room without speaking. That was on the second day of the sixth week after the release of Marin's tape.

On the morning of the third day of the sixth week after the release of Marin's tape Dickie called from Hollister to say that Warren was at the ranch.

"Acting crazy. Irrational. He told Linda that he talked to Leonard in Miami and Leonard said he could stay."

Charlotte said nothing.

"He yelled at Linda."

Charlotte said nothing.

"Obscenities."

Charlotte replaced the receiver and lay down on Marin's bed.

"You're aware Mark Schrader killed himself in Mexico," the reporter said on the telephone.

"Arizona," Charlotte said. She was still lying on Marin's bed. The sound of the man's voice hurt her ear and she held the receiver several inches away.

"About Mark and Marin——"

"Arizona. Not Mexico. He killed himself in Nogales, Arizona."

"Absolutely. My slip. Would you say that Marin was romantically involved with Mark?"

"Romantically involved," Charlotte repeated.

"Involved in a romantic way, yes."

The harelip's the fresh meat they'll throw on the trail, they can't afford him, Marin's not stupid.

I wouldn't rely on that.

"You see you're thinking of Nogales, Sonora," Charlotte said.

"Absolutely," the reporter said. "Very good. About Mark and——"

"You don't have to congratulate me. For knowing the difference between Arizona and Mexico."

"About Marin and—"

This is the worst behavior yet.

"Fuck Marin," Charlotte said.

"Because he was married to you," Leonard said when she called him in Miami. "That's why I told him he could stay at your fucking ranch. Because you kissed him goodbye at Idlewild and told him you'd be back in a week. Because he was Marin's father. And because I don't happen to believe it's Porter who is dying."

"Is Marin's father. *Is."*

"You didn't hear what I said. I said I don't happen to believe he's talking about anybody but himself."

There was a silence.

"I heard what you said," Charlotte said finally. "Tell me—"

"Tell you what."

"Tell me—"

"Tell you if you're not there when I get back I'll shoot myself?"

Charlotte said nothing.

"I won't. That's his game, not mine. I want you. I don't need you."

"If you think he's dying he's not," Charlotte said after a while. "If you're trying to say you think he's dying you're wrong."

Leonard said nothing.

"Something else you were wrong about," Charlotte said. "You said I'd leave you the same way I left him. I'm not. I'm leaving you. I'm telling you."

The rain was light and the dark came early and the traffic moved. By the time she arrived at the turnoff

to the Hollister ranch she was just ten months short of
the Boca Grande airport. El Aeropuerto del Presidente
General Luis Strasser-Mendana. My brother-in-law.
Deceased.

THREE

1

SHE HAD BEEN GOING TO ONE AIRPORT OR ANOTHER for four months, one could see it, looking at the visas on her passport. All those airports where Charlotte Douglas's passport had been stamped would have looked alike. Sometimes the sign on the tower would say "Bienvenidos" and sometimes the sign on the tower would say "Bienvenue," some places were wet and hot and others dry and hot, but at each of those airports the pastel concrete walls would rust and stain and the swamp off the runway would be littered with the fuselages of cannibalized Fairchild F-227's and the water would need boiling.

I knew why Charlotte went to the airport even if Victor did not.

I knew about airports.

People who go to the airport first invent some business to conduct there, a ticket to be adjusted, a query about cargo rates, a newspaper unavailable elsewhere. Then they convince themselves that the airport is cooler than the hotel, or has superior chicken salad.

Then one day they see a plane, "their" plane, one plane of many but somehow marked, a mirage on the tarmac.

They pay the lunch check.

They buy the ticket, they glance at the clock above the counter.

Quite as if they were ordinary travelers.

I supposed that one day Charlotte Douglas would be sitting in the Boca Grande airport and would see her plane and get on it, just as she had clearly gotten on her plane from New Orleans to Mérida and Mérida to Antigua and Antigua to Guadeloupe and Guadeloupe to Boca Grande, supposed that she would maintain that blind course south, but she never did.

2

LOOK AT THE VISAS. TRACE BACK THE COURSE.

Before Boca Grande she had been on Guadeloupe.
A few tourists had been killed by terrorists on
Guadeloupe that year and until the Air France crash
Charlotte was the only guest at the hotel, which had
been built just before the trouble and was very large
with open terraces where the rain splashed. Her clothes
mildewed. The untouched butter in the little crocks
went rancid by noon and by dinner was dusted with
the fine volcanic ash still falling from an eruption two
years before. One of the killings had taken place on
the dining terrace of the hotel, and there was a stub-
born bloodstain on the concrete at which a busboy
scrubbed desultorily every afternoon.

After the Paris–Lima flight hit the volcano there was
another woman at the hotel, the wife of the Air
France investigator, but she and Charlotte did not
speak. The woman was very small and tanned and she
played backgammon all day with the beach boys,
cheating and winning. Charlotte rented a Peugeot to

drive up the volcano but at the first turn she came upon
a large black plastic tarpaulin on which lay fragments
of metal and one teddy bear. As she drove back to the
hotel it occurred to Charlotte that Marin could have
been on that plane under a different name.

Marin could also have been on the Delta flight that
crashed at Dulles.

Marin could have been on the Alitalia that exploded
over the North Atlantic.

Marin was loose in the world and could leave it any
time and Charlotte would have no way of knowing.

Before Guadeloupe Charlotte had been on Antigua.

Winds blew on Antigua and she rarely left the hotel.
She was uncertain where the hotel even was, except
that it was a long way from the airport: she recalled
taxi rides through the cane and a small one-story hotel
on the water. Her skin burned in the wind and in the
odd glare off the opaque clouded sea and after the
first week she did not go outside. In the evenings Charlotte and the other off-season guests, two lesbians
from Toronto and for a while a man and a woman,
Seventh-Day Adventists from Newport Beach, California, were served conch stew at a single table by the
swimming pool. Perhaps because the man and the
woman from Newport Beach were not married to each
other or perhaps because as Seventh-Day Adventists
they did not approve of drinking they would appear
each night only when the plates were set on the table
and vanish directly after the Key Lime pie. For the
rest of the evening Charlotte would sit by the pool and
look at the illustrated books the manager pressed on
her, cheaply bound books with mildewed pages and
titles like *The Funeral of King George VI* and *The
Marriage of Princess Margaret,* and the lesbians would
get drunk on rum punches and dance to the Mabel

Mercer records they had brought from Toronto. They had made a new life in Toronto and they were thinking about making another new life on Antigua but they were both Americans and they had both gone to Miss Porter's School in Farmington, Connecticut.

"Not together," the younger one said. "Not at the same time we didn't."

"We were both at Farmington," the older one said.

"At different times." The younger one took Charlotte's hand and studied it. "You have a beautiful lifeline."

The older one wept.

Mabel Mercer sang "My Shining Hour."

Charlotte put down *The Marriage of Princess Margaret* and stared at the sea. She had the sense that she could swim from where she was to somewhere else, but she had no idea what lay out there, or in which direction she was staring. In any case she could not swim at night because she could not see the bottom. She remembered swimming at night with Marin on the reef off Waikiki and screaming when Marin's leg brushed hers.

Before Antigua Charlotte had been in Mérida.

Mérida was where she had taken the baby to die of complications, her baby, Leonard's baby, the baby she was carrying when she left California with Warren, the baby born prematurely, hydrocephalic, and devoid of viable liver function in the Ochsner Clinic in New Orleans. The doctors had said the baby would die in the hospital but it did not. It took a long time to die even in Mérida. She had taken the baby to Mérida because she thought it would die faster there but it did not. Toward the beginning of the two weeks she waited for the baby to die she moistened its lips with tap water and told it about the places they would see together.

They would of course see the Great Banyan at Calcutta.

They would see the stone slabs in the conservatory at Bangalore.

They would see the monkeys in the primeval garden at Singapore, they would see the Royal Palm Avenue at Peradeniya, due to reach its best appearance in the year 2050.

They would not see the cacti at San Marino. Marin had not minded the cacti at San Marino but Charlotte had. San Marino had given Charlotte bad dreams. Cacti. Fungi. Fat dry spikes. San Marino would give the baby bad dreams too.

"No San Marino," Charlotte promised the baby. "Quite frankly you wouldn't like it."

After a few days Charlotte exhausted her memory of botanical gardens around the world and began planning one for Mérida. She "named" everything around her. She asked the botanical names of all the plants outside the hotel in Mérida and listed them by genera and subgenera, made notations about color variation in seasonal blossoms, and engaged the manager of the hotel in an astonishing discussion of why he did not dedicate the parking lot to the cultivation of native flora; by the middle of the second week she had progressed from flora to fauna and was cataloguing the birds, the lizards, the insects that bred in the hotel plumbing and crawled from every drain in spite of daily flushings with Ortho-Muerte.

Typhoid was epidemic in the Yucatán that year but still the baby did not die.

By the end of the second week Charlotte was cataloguing the bacteria, the parasites, the sources of fever and intestinal infection: poinciana and poinsettia gave way to salmonella, another tropical flowering. The ight in Mérida when the diarrhea finally came Charlotte held the small warm dehydrating creature in her arms all night. Toward midnight she weakened, tried to charter a plane to take her back to New Orleans or even to Miami, but no one answered the telephone at the airport, and when Charlotte went out there by taxi with the baby in her arms she found only the controller playing cards with a couple of Yucatair mechanics and they said there were no charters in Mérida that night.

LEONARD HAD NOT WANTED HER TO SEE THE BABY but she had.

Leonard had wanted her to leave the baby to die in the Ochsner Clinic but she would not.

There had been words about it.

There had been words between Leonard and Warren about it in the room at the Ochsner Clinic but she could barely remember the words.

There had been words in the room at the Ochsner Clinic and there had also been peonies. She could remember the peonies very clearly and she could remember the words only barely and mainly she remembered that she had not wanted the baby to die without her.

The baby did not die at the Mérida airport but an hour later, in the parking lot of the Coca-Cola bottling plant on the road back into town. The baby had gone into convulsions and projectile vomiting in the taxi and Charlotte had made the driver stop in the parking lot. She walked with the baby on the dark asphalt. She sang to the baby out on the edge of the asphalt.

here the rushes grew and a few trailers were parked.
y the time the baby died the taxi had left but it was
nly a mile or two to the Centro Médico de Yucatán
nd Charlotte walked there with the baby in her arms,
usting at last, its vomit spent. The doctor did not
peak English but marked the death certificate in En-
lish: *death by complications*.

"Complications of what," Charlotte said.

"Complications of dying," the doctor said. "Her
ame in Christ?"

The Louisiana birth certificate said *Douglas, Baby
irl*. The Mexican tourist card said *Douglas, Infanta*.
eonard said *it*. Charlotte said *baby*.

"Charlotte," Charlotte said. "Her name is Char-
tte."

"Carlota," the doctor said, and made the sign of the
ross before he signed the certificate.

Carlota Douglas was buried in a short coffin which
e doctor's brother-in-law would not close until Char-
tte had inspected his work. He was very proud of the
ork he had done on the baby. He was very grateful
o have the job and he wanted Charlotte to be pleased.
Ie had wrapped the baby in a lavender nylon shawl
nd put a bow in her hair and tiny red shoes on her
eet. Charlotte had looked once and then away. She
ad paid the doctor and his brother-in-law in Amer-
can ten-dollar bills. Before she left Mérida she called
eonard in San Francisco and told him that the baby
as dead.

"I'll come get you if you want," Leonard had said.

"Whatever you want," Charlotte had said.

"You have to say."

"They put shoes on her feet. Red shoes."

"It's over. Forget it. You never should have seen it.
You never should have."

"Warren's not responsible. For my coming down here. If that's what you think."

"No," Leonard had said. "That's not what I think."

"I think I better call you back later," Charlotte had said, but she had not called Leonard back later.

She had not called Leonard back later and she had not called Warren at all.

In the evening before the plane left for Antigua she had gone back to the cemetery and tried to find the baby's grave but she could not. It was not a large cemetery but there seemed to be a large number of small fresh unmarked graves. She left the bougainvillea she had torn from the wall of the hotel on one of them.

FOUR

1

Fevers relapse here.

Bacteria proliferate.

Termites eat the presidential palace, rust eats my Oldsmobile.

Twice a year the sun is exactly vertical, and nothing casts a shadow.

The bite of one fly deposits an egg which in its pupal stage causes human flesh to suppurate.

The bite of another deposits a larval worm which three years later surfaces on and roams the human eyeball.

Everything here changes and nothing appears to. There is no perceptible wheeling of the stars in their courses, no seasonal wane in the length of the days or the temperature of air or earth or water, only the amniotic stillness in which transformations are constant. As elsewhere, certain phases in these transformations are called by certain names ("Oldsmobile," say, and "rust"), but the emotional field of such names tends to weaken as one leaves the temperate zones. At the equator the names are noticeably arbitrary. A banana palm is no more or less "alive" than its rot.

Is it.

I tried to tell Charlotte this but once again Charlotte did not quite see my point.

Charlotte did not take the equatorial view.

Of anything that had happened.

Charlotte did not even remember much of what had happened during the six months between leaving California with Warren and taking the baby to Mérida. She remembered certain days and nights very clearly but she did not remember their sequence. Someone had shuffled her memory. Certain cards were lost. She and Warren had been in the South. She knew that much. They had been in New Orleans a while in January and February, and then again when it was hot and raining and the baby was showing, she remembered that. She remembered arriving at the New Orleans airport. The airport must have been in January because the second time they arrived in New Orleans, the time it was hot and raining and the baby was showing and the girl was with them, they had not flown in but driven in, from Greenville. They had eaten some crab bisque once in Greenville. They had made that crab bisque in Greenville. She had bought the crabs and Warren had shown her how to make the bisque.

"You're ruining it," she had said. "You're putting in too much salt."

"You don't know anything about it."

"Taste it, it's brine."

"Taste it yourself," Warren had said, and pushed the wooden spoon in her face. The soup had gone up her nose and she had choked and he had hit her between the shoulder blades until she stopped. "I never cared for anybody like I cared for you but you never knew your ass about food."

Everyone else had liked that crab bisque but they had stayed too long in Greenville, they had stayed too long everywhere. After-three-days-guests-like-fish-begin-to-stink. She had heard that all over the South with Warren. After three weeks of hearing it from Howard Hollerith in Greenville she and Warren had moved from Howard Hollerith's place to a motel in town near the levee but Warren had kept on seeing Howard Hollerith's wife. And Howard Hollerith's girl too. The wife and the girl. "I want them to do it together," Warren said to Charlotte. The girl went to New Orleans with them.

But Greenville was May, June. She knew that Greenville was May or June because Birmingham was July.

The Mountain Brook Country Club in Birmingham was definitely July.

The New Orleans airport had been January.

Warren had been drunk and had twisted her arm behind her back at the Hertz counter.

"I don't have to be here," she had said. "I'm going home."

"Go home," Warren had said. "I'll send you home. I'll ask Porter for the fare, go into debt and send you home. How do you think you're going home without sending me into debt."

"The way I came," Charlotte said, and Warren had hit her.

"It's all right," Charlotte kept saying to the Hertz girl, and "No. Don't call. Please don't." The Hertz girl was calling the airport police and Warren was buying a postcard and mailing it to Leonard. The postcard showed a Confederate flag and a mule and the legend

PUT YOUR *HEART* IN DIXIE OR GET YOUR *ASS* OUT. "It's all right," Charlotte said to the airport police. "It's nothing, it's personal, it's all right."

Delta had lost her bags but it did not seem to matter.

"You forgot your map," the Hertz girl said.

"Lower that white-trash voice," Warren said.

In the Hertz car they had driven from the airport to Porter's new house in Metairie and it began to appear that Leonard had been right again. Porter did not appear to be dying but Warren did. Porter told her that. Porter told her that while Warren was upstairs calling a girl he knew in Savannah and telling her to come down. Porter hoped that Charlotte would understand why she and Warren could not stay with him. Porter hoped that she would not think it inhospitable for him to have made a reservation for her and Warren at the Pontchartrain. By the way, the reservation would be in her name because the last time Warren had stayed at the Pontchartrain there had been a little unpleasantness, Porter would not say what.

"Warren doesn't show his best side as a houseguest, Charlotte, you recognize that. If Warren has to leave us, I want to recall his many virtues only."

"What do you mean, leave us."

"About time he came home, stopped catting around New York. 'Dying Is But Going Home,' am I right? Ever hear that?"

"What are you talking about, dying."

"Used to see it on gravestones. 'Dying Is But Going Home.' 'The Angels Called Him,' that was popular too. At least around here it was popular. I don't know about out there."

"You said if Warren 'has to leave us,' Porter, what did you mean?"

"Don't bother yourself, Charlotte. I'm going to persuade Warren to let Ping Walker have a look, you remember Ping, Lady Duvall's boy? Lived up east a while? Came back down home around the time Lady married her fancy man?"

"I don't know any Ping Walker and I don't know any Lady Duvall and I don't see what they've got to do with Warren."

"Don't raise your voice, Charlotte, your husband out there allow you to converse like a fishwife? Ping is a specialist. I should say, a specialist. Very fine training. Tulane, Hopkins, Harvard. His father didn't pay for it, old Judge Duvall did."

"A specialist in what?"

"Bad blood," Warren said from the stairway, and both he and Porter laughed.

"Bad blood between Warren here and Lady's fancy man, if memory serves."

"Watch your mouth," Warren said.

"Porter said you were sick."

She was standing at the window in the room at the Pontchartrain watching the first light on the windows of the houses across the avenue. She did not have a bag, she did not have an aspirin, she did not have a toothbrush. The skirt she had put on the morning before in Hollister was wrinkled from the long drive to the San Francisco airport and the long flight to New Orleans and the long night watching Warren and Porter drink in Metairie. In a few hours she could go out and buy what she needed. She tried to concentrate on what she needed and did not think about what she was doing in a room at the Pontchartrain Hotel on St. Charles Avenue in New Orleans. In the empty house on California Street in San Francisco it would be three o'clock in the morning. The night light in Marin's bathroom would be burning just as she had left it. The crossed spots on the Pollock in the dining room would be burning just as she had left them. Leonard would have gone on by now from Miami to Havana via Mexico City. Leonard was in Havana and Marin was gone. Warren was either dying or not dying and Marin was gone.

"Porter said you were sick and he wasn't. At all."

"Porter's an ass, don't you be one." Warren lay on the bed and unbuttoned his shirt. "You got it wrong. As usual. Shut those curtains and come here."

We could have been doing this all our lives, Warren said.

We should be doing this all our lives, Warren said.

We should have done this all our lives, we should do this all our lives.

The verb form made a difference and she could not get it straight what Warren had said. She could not remember. She could remember the New Orleans airport and she could remember the Mountain Brook Country Club in Birmingham but she could not remember too much in between. There must have been about five months in between, about twenty weeks, about 140 days, simple arithmetic told her how many days there must have been between the New Orleans airport and the Mountain Brook Country Club in Birmingham, but someone had shuffled them. Everywhere she had been with him he wanted the curtains shut in the daylight, she did remember that. She remembered darkened rooms with the light cracking through where the curtains were skimpy and all she could not remember was where those rooms were, or why she and Warren had been in them.

"You wanted to bring me home with you," she

remembered saying in one of them. "Didn't you. You wanted to come home again."

"No," Warren had said. "I just wanted to fuck you again."

Sometimes those months in the South seemed so shattered that she suspected the Ochsner Clinic of having administered electroshock while she was under the anaesthesia for delivery. This suspicion was unfounded.

2

I SAID BEFORE HE HAD THE LOOK OF A MAN WHO could drive a woman like Charlotte right off her head.

His face had been coarsened by contempt.

His mind had been coarsened by self-pity.

As it happened he was quite often "right" to hold other people in contempt, and he was also "right" to regard himself with pity, but allow a dying woman a maxim or two.

I have noticed that it is never enough to be right.

I have noticed that it is necessary to be better.

His favorite hand was outrageousness; in a fluid world like Leonard Douglas's where no one could be outraged Warren Bogart was dimmed, confused, unable to operate. He could operate marginally in academe, and he maintained vague academic connections: a week at Yale, three days at Harvard, guest privileges at a number of Faculty Clubs where he never paid his bar bill. He could operate marginally on the Upper East Side of New York. He could operate very well in the South. Like many Southerners and like some Catholics and unlike Charlotte he was raised to believe not in "hard work" or "self-reliance" but in the infinite power of the personal appeal, the request for a favor, the intervention of one or another merciful Virgin. He had an inchoate but definite conviction that access to the mysteries of good fortune was arranged in the same way as access to the Boston Club, a New Orleans institution to which he did not belong but always had a guest card.

He belonged to nothing.

He was an outsider who lived by his ability to manipulate the inside.

His final hold on Charlotte was that he recognized in himself everything I have just told you about him, and said *mea culpa*.

As another outsider I recognized that hand too.

Outsider. *De afuera.*

We were both *de afuera*, Warren Bogart and I. At the time I met him we were also both dying of cancer, Warren Bogart and I, which perhaps made us even more *de afuera* than usual, but that was a detail Charlotte had never made entirely clear.

Charlotte had trouble with the word.

Not the word "cancer."

The word "dying."

I met him only once, one evening in New Orleans four or five months after Charlotte first came to Boca Grande, one evening in the Garden District at the house of one of the fat brothers in white suits who factor our copra. I had flown to New Orleans that morning to receive cobalt and to renegotiate the copra contracts with Morgan Fayard; I was due to have dinner with Morgan and his wife and sister and to fly back to Boca Grande the next morning. I had not been invited to dinner to meet Warren Bogart, nor had Warren Bogart been invited at all. He was just there in Morgan and Lucy Fayard's living room when I arrived. He was a visible thorn in Lucy Fayard's plan for the evening. He seemed bent on embarrassing both Lucy and her sister-in-law Adele, as well as on humiliating the girl he had with him, but the central thrust of his visit seemed to be to see me. This girl he had with him was referred to as "Chrissie," or "Miss Bailey," or "our unexpected guest's little friend from Tupelo," depending on who referred to her, and she was thin and pale and spoke, when prodded, in sporadic and obscurely startling monologues. In fact she was not unlike Charlotte Douglas, give or take twenty years and the distinctions in cultural conditioning between Tupelo, Mississippi, and Hollister, California. Still I watched the two of them in the Fayards' living room for several minutes before I understood that this "Warren" who had arrived uninvited for drinks and would stay unasked through dinner and who studied my every reaction was the Warren who figured in what I had come to regard as Charlotte Douglas's hallucinations.

"Just so thoughtful of you to drop by, Warren." Lucy Fayard's voice carried clear and thin as glass. "Morgan and I long to have you for a whole evening one time soon. You and your friend. You're most definitely included, Miss Bailey."

The girl from Tupelo smiled wanly and tied on a scarf as if instructed to make her goodbyes.

"Here's-your-hat-what's-your-hurry." Warren Bogart held out his glass to be filled. "Take that bandana off, Chrissie, don't mind your hostess. Mrs. Fayard's been learning West Texas manners."

"Just shush about that," Lucy Fayard said.

"Just don't start about that," Adele Fayard said.

"Lucy doesn't associate with West Texas trash," Morgan Fayard said. "I don't allow Adele to filthy this house with him. Grace doesn't know what we're talking about and it's rude to continue, in fact I forbid it."

As a matter of fact I knew precisely what they were talking about, because the last evening I had spent with the Fayards had been devoted exclusively to a heated discussion of this same "West Texas trash." It had appeared then that Adele Fayard was seeing a man from Midland of whom her brother did not approve. It appeared now that Lucy Fayard was seeing him as well, and that Morgan did not yet know it. Very soon now either Lucy or Adele would allude to one of Morgan's own indiscretions. All evenings with the Fayards were essentially Caribbean, volatile with conflicting pieties and intimations of sexual perfidy, and in that context were neither very difficult to understand nor, in the end, very engaging.

"That West Texas trash doesn't enter this house," Morgan Fayard said, ignoring his own injunction.

"My mistake then," Warren Bogart said. "I thought I met him here."

"I should say, your mistake," Lucy Fayard said.

"You are certainly set on making it difficult, Warren." Adele Fayard smiled. "Just as difficult as can be."

"Set on making what difficult, Adele."

"You know perfectly well what's difficult, Warren."

"Difficult for you and your discourteous sister-in-law to continue to extend me your famous hospitality during my dying days? That about it, Adele? Or is it my mistake again."

"What dying days you talking about," Morgan Fayard said. "Nobody dying here."

"You're all dying. You're dying, your wife and sister are dying, your little children are dying, Chrissie here is dying, even Miss Tabor there is dying."

Warren Bogart watched me as he lit a cigar. I had not been introduced to him as Grace Tabor.

"But not one of you is dying as fast as I'm dying." Warren Bogart smiled. "Which I believe allows me certain privileges."

"Frankly he didn't behave any better when he wasn't dying," Adele Fayard said.

"Frankly it's not ennobling him one bit," Lucy Fayard said.

The girl from Tupelo laughed nervously.

" 'Sunset and evening star and one clear call for me!' " Morgan Fayard cried suddenly. " 'And let there be no mourning at the bar when I put out to sea.' Learned that at Charlottesville."

"Not any too well," Warren Bogart said.

"No mourning at the bar, Warren. Lesson there for all of us."

"It's 'moaning of' the bar, Morgan. Not 'mourning at' the bar. It's not a wake in one of those gin mills you frequent."

"I don't guess George Gordon Lord Byron is going to object."

"Wrong again, Morgan. You don't guess Alfred Lord Tennyson is going to object. You recite it, Chrissie. Stand up and recite. Recite that and 'Thanatopsis' both."

The girl looked at him pleadingly.

"Stand up," Warren Bogart said.

"I must say," Lucy Fayard said.

"Shut up, Lucy. I said stand up, Chrissie."

The girl from Tupelo stood up and gazed miserably at the floor.

"Speak up now, or I'll make you do 'Evangeline' too."

" 'Sunset and evening star—And one clear call for me—And may there be no—' "

The girl's voice was low and wretched.

Warren Bogart picked up his drink and walked over to me.

"It is Miss Tabor, isn't it?"

" 'Twilight and evening bell—And after that the dark—' "

The girl was speaking with her eyes shut. All three Fayards sat as if frozen.

"It was," I said finally.

"I believe you did research of some sort with my old friend Mr. McKay. In Peru."

"In Brazil." At the end of each line the girl would open her eyes and look at Warren Bogart's back as if he alone could save her. "If you're talking about Claude McKay it was Brazil."

"Somewhere down there, you may be right."

"I am right. I was there. What exactly are you doing to that child."

"Chrissie? Chrissie's brilliant, you should talk to her, she's very interested in anthropology, took some courses in it at Newcomb. Does some homework before she speaks. Mr. McKay would have been devoted to her. He had a place in Maryland, you probably know it, I used to drink with him there before he died." He glanced across the room at the girl, who had fallen silent. "Straighten those shoulders, Chrissie, don't slouch. 'Thanatopsis' now."

" 'To him who in the love of nature holds—Communion with her visible forms—' "

The girl's voice was so low as to be inaudible.

"Would have been devoted to her," Warren Bogart

repeated. "May he rest in peace. An American aristo-crat, Claude McKay. One of the last. Gentleman. Well-born, well-bred."

The evening was hot. I was tired. When I am tired I remember what I was taught in Colorado. When I remember what I was taught in Colorado certain words set my teeth on edge. "Aristocrat" is one of those words. "Gentleman" is another. They remind me of that strain I dislike in Gerardo. As a child Gerardo once described the father of a classmate as "in trade" and I slapped his face.

"Last of a breed," Warren Bogart said, watching my face. "Used to speak about you. You should meet my good friend Miss Tabor, he'd say."

The last time I could recall seeing Claude McKay I had accused him of publishing my work under his name. I wondered when Warren Bogart would get around to Charlotte.

"I never thought I'd run into you here at Lucy's," he said.

I have never had patience with games.

"I expect you did," I said.

The girl from Tupelo had finished reciting. The room was silent. Warren Bogart was fingering his cigar and watching me warily.

"Warren," the girl said. "I finished. I'm through."

"Do 'Snowbound,'" Warren Bogart said. "There's nobody here wouldn't be improved by hearing 'Snow-bound.'"

"I just won't allow this," Lucy Fayard said.

"I'd advise you to save that tone of voice for West Texas," Warren Bogart said.

"What's this he's saying about West Texas," Morgan Fayard said.

"Just nonsense, Bro." Adele Fayard stood up. "He's talking nonsense."

"I'm asking certain people in this room a question, Adele." Morgan Fayard pushed his sister back into her chair with the heel of his hand. "And I believe I'm owed the courtesy of a reply."

"What's the question, Bro?"

"God*damn* West Texas trash."

The girl from Tupelo began to cry.

Dinner was announced.

No one moved.

"This is a fucking circus. A freak show." Warren Bogart turned to me. "Doesn't this put you in mind of some third-rate traveling circus? Some Sells-Floto circus passing through that country you people run so well? Doesn't it?"

"No," I said. "It puts me in mind of the Mountain Brook Country Club in Birmingham, Alabama."

Warren Bogart looked at me and then away. "You're in over your head," he said finally, and that was all he said.

Trout was served in the dining room. Lemon mousse was served in the dining room. Coffee and praline cookies and pear brandy were served in the dining room. The dining room was hot and we could not seem to leave it. Lucy and Adele Fayard described their most recent Junior League project in compulsive detail. Lucy and Adele Fayard described dinner as we ate it. Lucy and Adele Fayard described a pet cobra they had seen drink Wild Turkey-and-water at a party the night before.

"I told Morgan," Lucy Fayard said, " 'Look there, Morgan, I believe that cobra is taking some *drinks*.' "

"I said to Morgan," Adele Fayard said, " 'Mark my

words, Morgan, that cobra's going to have itself a *season* in New Orleans.' "

Morgan Fayard sulked. Warren Bogart remained in the living room with the girl from Tupelo. We could hear them at the piano. Warren Bogart seemed to be making the girl play, over and over again, the song that was always played in New Orleans at Mardi Gras. She played it badly.

" '*May the fish get legs and the cows lay—*' That's an A-flat, Chrissie, you missed the flat. Start over."

"*Dare* he sing that song," Morgan Fayard said.

Lucy Fayard raised her voice. "You're forgetting your duties, Morgan. Grace's glass is empty. You ever get ground artichokes down there, Grace? To put around game?"

"Not forgetting *my* duties," Morgan Fayard muttered. "Fine one to talk."

" '*May the fish get legs and the cows lay eggs—If ever I cease to love—May all dogs wag their—*' No. No, Chrissie. No."

"The *irony*," Morgan Fayard said. "You talking about *duties*."

"We should ship some down to you," Lucy Fayard said. "Ground artichokes. To put around game. Morgan. Grace's glass."

"Actually," I said. "I have to leave."

"See now what you've done, Morgan. Making us all suffer at this stuffy table instead of taking our coffee in the living room like civilized beings, no wonder Grace wants to leave."

"Not going out there to be insulted," Morgan Fayard said.

" '*May the fish get legs and the cows lay eggs—If ever I cease to love—May all dogs wag their tails in front—*' "

172

"Got no *right* to sing that song," Morgan Fayard said.

"He has too a right," Lucy Fayard said. "He's from here."

"Not from here at all. He's from—" Morgan Fayard spit the words out. "Plaquemines Parish. That's where he's from. Where he left a—"

"I don't guess Mardi Gras is your own personal property," Lucy Fayard said. "Just because your mother was Queen of Comus. Which Adele, incidentally, was not."

"—Where he no doubt left a promising future as assistant manager of a gasoline station, that's the kind of trash you—"

I stood up.

Something about the presence of Warren Bogart was causing the Fayards to outdo even themselves.

"You back on West Texas?" Lucy Fayard said. "Or you still on Warren."

"It's a tacky song anyway," Adele Fayard said. "Mardi Gras comes, I go out of town with the Jews. Do sit down, Grace."

"I won't tolerate this." Morgan Fayard slammed his fist on the table. "I will not tolerate having my little children exposed to this trash."

"Unless I'm very much mistaken your little children are at school in Virginia," Adele Fayard said. "Which makes your tolerance the slightest bit academic?"

"I been hearing certain things about you in the Quarter," I could hear Morgan Fayard saying as I left the dining room. "Sister."

"I understand you've been leaving your own visiting cards at a certain address in the Quarter," I could hear Adele Fayard saying as I walked through the living room. "Bro."

" '*May the fish get legs and the cows lay eggs—If ever I cease to love—May the moon be turned to green cream cheese—If ever I cease to love—May the—*' "

Warren Bogart looked up from the piano.

"Pretty little song, isn't it."

I said nothing.

"Tell Charlotte she was wrong," he said.

3

HERE AMONG THE THREE OR FOUR SOLVENT FAM-
ilies in Boca Grande we have specific traditional treat-
ments for specific traditional complaints. Nausea is
controlled locally by a few drops of 1:1000 solution of
adrenalin in a little water, taken by mouth with sips
of iced champagne. Neurasthenia is controlled locally
by a half-grain of phenobarbitone three times a day
and temporary removal to a hill station. In the absence of a hill Miami or Caracas will suffice. I have
never known a treatment specific to the condition in
which Charlotte Douglas arrived in Boca Grande, but
after that one meeting with her first husband I began
to see a certain interior logic in her inability to remember much about those last months she spent with
him.

One thing she did remember was when and where
she left him.

"I don't want to leave you ever," she remembered
saying to him in Biloxi.

175

"How could I leave you," she remembered saying to him in Meridian.

She left him at ten minutes past eleven P.M. on the eighteenth of July in the bar of the Mountain Brook Country Club in Birmingham.

I'm dizzy and my head hurts, the girl had said.

I think she should see a doctor, Charlotte had said.

She doesn't need a doctor, Warren had said. She's drunk and she needs a sandwich.

Sometime in the next several minutes, at the very moment when Warren hit both the waiter and Minor Clark, Charlotte got up from the table and walked in the direction of the ladies' room and kept walking. She did not risk waiting to call a taxi. She just walked. She had been wearing a sweater in the bar but the night outside was hot and she dropped the sweater in a sand trap and kept walking. Once she was off the golf course she paused at each intersection to assess the size of the houses and the probable cost of their upkeep and then she walked in whichever direction the houses seemed smaller, the lawns less clipped. She had a fixed idea that she would not be safe until she had reached a part of town where people sat on their porches and on the fenders of parked cars and would be bored enough to take her side if Warren came after her. When it began to rain her feet slipped in her sandals and she took off her sandals and walked barefoot. She knew exactly what time it had been when she left the Mountain Brook Country Club because Minor Clark had said the girl did not need a sandwich, she needed a doctor, and Warren had ordered a sandwich and the waiter had said it was ten minutes past eleven and the kitchen was closed. So she had left the Mountain Brook Country Club at ten minutes past eleven and it was almost one before she came to a part of town so rundown she felt safe enough to stand in a lighted place and call a taxi.

The girl's name was Julia Erskine.

The girl was not whining as Warren said but crying because her head hurt. Charlotte believed that Julia Erskine's head hurt.

The girl said that her head hurt because she had fallen from a horse that morning while riding with Warren. Charlotte did not believe that Julia Erskine had fallen from a horse that morning while riding with Warren.

When the taxi came Charlotte went to the Birmingham airport. The first plane out was for New Orleans and Charlotte got on it. She was the only passenger. "You and I can watch the sunrise," the stewardess said. Charlotte did not feel safe until the plane was airborne and then she ordered a drink and sat with her head against the cold window and did not watch the sunrise but drank the bourbon very fast before the ice could dilute it. She had not eaten since lunch the day before at Minor and Suzanne Clark's, the lunch at Minor and Suzanne Clark's to which Julia Erskine and Warren had never come, and as the bourbon hit her stomach she was pleasantly astonished with herself.

She was pleasantly astonished that she could still do all these things.

Walk out.

Call a taxi.

Use her American Express card, get on a plane, order a drink.

While she was still being pleasantly astonished her water broke, and soaked the seat with amniotic fluid.

"You hurt that girl," Charlotte said to Warren when he brought the peonies to the Ochsner Clinic.

Leonard was in the room. Charlotte did not know how Leonard happened to be in the room and she knew that she should not say anything about the girl in front of Leonard but it did not seem to matter any more what she said in front of anyone. "You hit her in the head. Didn't you."

"She's doped up," Leonard said. "Stay neutral."

"Don't talk about things you don't know about," Warren said to Charlotte. "What are you going to do about the baby?"

"Just the note I had in mind," Leonard said.

"How did you find me," Charlotte said.

"Never mind how I found you. I always find you. What about the baby."

"The baby is—you hit that girl in the head."

"You're on pills," Warren said. "You don't know what you're talking about."

"Don't let that stop you," Leonard said. "Pitch her another life decision."

"He doesn't want you to see the baby," Warren said. "Does he."

"No," Leonard said. "I don't. The topic is now closed. Now we're going to limit our remarks to areas in which Charlotte has no immediate interest. Sex. Politics. Religion. All right?"

"You don't know anything about Charlotte," Warren said. Charlotte could smell bay rum. Bay rum and cigar smoke. Warren. "You never did."

Charlotte tried to focus on the tight pink balls of peony blossom.

"He wants you to walk away," Warren said.

The tight pink balls seemed to swell as she watched them. The baby's head would swell if the baby lived but the baby could not live. They had told her so. The doctors. Leonard too. If Leonard had told her about the baby then Leonard had been in the room before, she had just forgotten.

"He wants you to walk away from here the same way you walked away from everything else in your life."

"You hit that girl in the head. You don't take care of anybody."

"I'm taking care of you right now. I'm telling you not to walk away."

"I never did," Charlotte said.

" 'How could I leave you,' " Warren said. "The same way you left everybody. How-could-I-leave-you-let-me-count-the-ways."

She closed her eyes against the obscene peonies.

"Never mind whether I take care of you," Warren said. "You can take care of me."

"Cut her loose," Leonard said.

"She doesn't want to be loose," Warren said.

The peonies were swelling behind her eyelids.

"It doesn't matter whether you take care of somebody or somebody takes care of you," Warren said. "It's the same thing in the end. It's all the same."

"You had your shot," Leonard said.

She kept her eyes closed and she heard their voices ugly and raised and by the time the voices were normal again the peonies had burst behind her eyelids and the warm drugs were pulling her back under and she knew what she was going to do. She was not going to do what they wanted her to do. She was not even sure what they wanted her to do but she was not going to do it.

"Tell her I said it's all the same," she heard Warren say to Leonard.

She was going to leave here alone with her baby.

"You want her to watch you die," she heard Leonard say to Warren.

She was going to let her baby die with her.

"Never mind what I want," she heard Warren say to Leonard. "Just tell her I said it's all the same. Tell her that for me."

4

WHEN I CONSIDER THE PATTERN OF THEIR DAYS and nights during those five months I see again that nothing outside that pattern happened at the Mountain Brook Country Club.

I wonder again why Charlotte left that night and not some other.

Charlotte could never tell me.

"But I had to leave," Charlotte would repeat, as if until ten minutes past eleven P.M. on the eighteenth of July there had been some imperative to her staying. "He'd been with this girl and he'd hurt her and he was acting crazy. After I left the Clarks took her to the hospital, she had a concussion. Mild."

Had not other such evenings occurred during those five months?

Charlotte said that she could not remember.

Bear in mind that I am talking here about a woman I believe to have been in shock.

Everywhere they went during those five months they ended up staying in a motel. Charlotte did remember the motels. They had stayed a while with Howard Hollerith in Greenville and they had stayed a while with Billy Daikin in Clarksdale and they had stayed a while with other people in other places but after a certain kind of evening they would always move to a motel. Usually Warren would not be present during the early part of this certain kind of evening. Usually Warren would be upriver or downriver or across the country with their host's wife or sister or recently divorced niece. Never daughter. Warren never went upriver or downriver or across the county with the daughter of a host.

Charlotte learned early to recognize the advent of such an evening.

For the day or two before such an evening Warren would announce his inability to sleep.

"I'm restless, I'm wired, I got the mean reds," he would say.

"Don't cross me," he would say.

"Don't mess with me," he would say.

For the day or two before such an evening their host would announce his inability to provide minor but key aspects of his normal hospitality.

"Wouldn't be surprised Warren's used up all those Peychaud bitters he can't take a drink without, what a shame, can't buy them up here."

"Damn that plumber, can't get here before Tuesday, daresay you'll be glad to get somewhere they've got the pipes in working order."

A familiar drift would emerge. Not only toilets but guest-room telephones would go out of order. Men would arrive to drain the swimming pool. Suggestions would be made for traveling before the rain set in, or the heat, or the projected work on the Interstate. Reminders would be made about promises to visit

Charlie Ferris in Oxford, or Miss Anne Clary on the Gulf.

Doors would be closed.

Voices would be raised.

The evening itself would begin uneasily and end badly.

"Hope Warren has the courtesy to leave a little something for old Jennie, all the extra picking up she's done, you might remind him, Charlotte. Or isn't that the custom where you come from."

And: "Most interesting the way men where you come from allow their wives to traipse around as they please, must be very advanced thinkers in California."

And then: "The idea, your friend Warren going off and leaving you here alone, might not matter to you but it matters to me, a man insults a lady in my house he insults me. You wouldn't understand that, Mrs. Douglas, I'm certain it's all free and easy where your people come from."

And finally: "You say you're going to bed 'and fuck it,' Mrs. Douglas, I believe that is your name, just what am I meant to conclude? Am I meant to conclude there's a woman in my house who's certifiable? Or did my ears deceive me."

After Charlotte went to bed there would be silence for a few hours and then more raised voices, Warren's among them, and Charlotte would bury her head in one pillow and put another over her belly so the baby could not hear and the next day she and Warren would move to a motel.

"I don't like these people," she said to Warren after one such evening. "I don't like them and I don't want to be beholden to them."

"You're not beholden to anybody. You're too used

to Arabs and Jews, you don't know how normal people behave."

"I can't help noticing Arabs and Jews are rather less insulting to their houseguests."

"Not to this houseguest they wouldn't be, babe." In the wreckage of these visits Warren seemed unfailingly cheerful. "You show me an Arab who'll put up with me, I'll show you an Arab who doesn't get the picture."

In all those motels he wanted the curtains shut in the daytime.

In all those motels she would sit in the dark room a while and watch him sleep.

It seemed to her that toward the end of the five months they had spent more time in motels than toward the beginning of the five months but she could not be sure. Warren always paid for the rooms with crumpled bills fished from various of his pockets and she paid for meals, when they ate meals. She ate regularly, usually alone. She forced herself to eat, just as she forced herself to take her calcium and see an obstetrician in any town where they spent more than a day or two. There was no need for her to see an obstetrician that often but she wanted to have a number she could call in the middle of the night. An obstetrician would not question her reason for seeing him. An obstetrician was the logical doctor to see.

"You're sick," she had said the first time she saw Warren gray and sweating. He had swerved abruptly off the highway and stopped the car on the shoulder. "You're sick and you need a doctor."

"Not going running to any doctor." His breathing was harsh and shallow and he did not seem to have strength to turn off the ignition. "Not sick. Ran over a moccasin is all."

They sat in the idling car until his breathing evened

out. He did not speak again but took her hand. When he finally put the car into gear and drove on she glanced back at the highway but of course there was no moccasin. It was after that day when she began to find an obstetrician in every town, began to get the questions done with early and the telephone number in hand. Some night in some town she was going to need to call a doctor and ask him for something and she wanted that doctor to take her call. She did not let her mind form the word "cancer" and she did not let her mind form the word "dying" but the word Demerol was always in her mind. She had not been there when her father died but Pete Wright had told her about the Demerol, the night they had dinner at the Palm.

5

SOMETIMES SHE WOULD LEAVE THE MOTEL DURING the day. She would leave Warren sleeping and take the car and drive down the main street of whatever town it was and look for somewhere to spend an hour. She remembered sitting in the library in Demopolis, Alabama, every afternoon for most of a week. She had read back newspapers in the Demopolis library. She had followed the progress in the newspapers of a Greene County murder trial which had taken place some months before. They left Demopolis before she got to the verdict and when she asked the woman at the motel desk if she recalled how the trial came out the woman said curiosity killed the cat. She remembered having her nails manicured in a pine town above Mobile by a child who looked like Marin but was fifteen and married to a logger and running her mother's beauty shop in a trailer. She remembered drinking chocolate Cokes at the counter of the Trailways station in Pass Christian and reading an Associated Press story about the continuing search for Marin Bogart and she remembered leaving the paper on the counter and staring out at the dark glare off the Gulf. She remembered drinking chocolate Cokes at the counter of the Trailways station in a lot of towns. She remembered staring at the Gulf in a lot of towns. She remembered the Associated Press quoting Leonard as saying that she was "traveling with friends."

On those days when she did leave the motel she would usually come back toward sundown and find Warren gone, the bed unmade, the towels wet on the floor of the room, the curtains still closed and the air sweet and heavy with the smell of bay rum. Warren never put the top back on the bottle of bay rum. She remembered that. She would put the top back on the bottle of bay rum and call the maid and stand outside on the walkway while the room was made up. The air would be chilly and wet and then later in the spring it would be warm and wet. Toward eight or nine on those evenings Warren would telephone the motel and tell her where to meet him.

"Warren appears to have his mood upon him," someone would be saying wherever she met him.

"Warren is certainly himself tonight."

"Warren is incorrigible."

"Warren is without doubt the most incorrigible of anybody I know."

So self-absorbed was the texture of life in these rooms where Charlotte went to meet Warren that the facts that she had been married to him for some years and that they were the parents of a child whose photograph appeared somewhere in every post office and gas station in the county appeared not to have penetrated.

She was Warren's "friend from California."

She was "visiting with Warren."

Warren was "showing Mrs. Douglas the South."

"Why do you lie?" Charlotte said after one such evening. "Why do you pretend I'm just this pregnant acquaintance you happen to be showing around Biloxi?"

"I'm not lying. You're just here on a visit. You'll leave."

"That's not what you make me say in bed."

"Don't talk about what I make you say in bed. Don't talk about it, talk about it and you lose it, don't you know anything."

We could have been doing this all our lives, Warren had said.

We should be doing this all our lives, Warren had said.

We should have done this all our lives, we should do this all our lives.

"I don't want to leave you ever," Charlotte said.

"No," Warren said. "But you will."

After a while there were no more frosts at night and the wild carrot came out along all the roads and every night ended badly.

After a while there were no more tule fogs at dawn and all Charlotte wanted was one night that did not end badly.

After a while there was Howard Hollerith's girl.

"What do you suppose Marin did today," Charlotte said one night in the car when she thought Howard Hollerith's girl was asleep in the back seat.

"Played tennis," Warren said. "Marin played tennis today."

"Marin who?" Howard Hollerith's girl said.

"See what you're going to leave me to," Warren said to Charlotte.

In the coffee shop of a Holiday Inn outside New

Orleans one morning in May or June Charlotte read another Associated Press story in which Leonard was again quoted as saying that Charlotte was "traveling with friends." This time Charlotte read the story several times and memorized the phrase. It occurred to her that possibly she had misunderstood the situation. Possibly Leonard and Warren and the Associated Press were right. She was simply traveling with friends, and Warren and Howard Hollerith's girl, asleep in the bed behind the second door past the ice machine, were simply the friends with whom she was traveling. Soothed by this construction Charlotte had another cup of coffee and worked the crossword in the *Picayune*.

6

THE LAST THING CHARLOTTE REMEMBERED BEFORE the Mountain Brook Country Club in Birmingham was sitting and reading inside the cyclone fence around the swimming pool at a Howard Johnson's in Meridian. The Howard Johnson's was just off a curve on the Interstate between New York and New Orleans and all afternoon the big northern rigs would appear to hurtle toward the cyclone fence and then veer on south. The vibration made her teeth hurt. The shallow end of the pool was filled with prematurely thickened young girls celebrating a forthcoming marriage. They talked as if they were just a year or two out of high school but they were already matrons, careful not to splash one another's blown and lacquered hair. After a while the bridegroom-to-be arrived with a friend from his office. The bridegroom and his friend were both fleshy young men in short-sleeved white shirts and they placed two six-packs of beer on a damp metal table and they opened all the cans and started drinking the beer. It seemed to be a town in which everyone thickened early.

Out of some deference or indifference to their own women the men ignored the shrieks from the pool and instead watched Charlotte as they drank the beer. "Somebody's gone and put a bun in that skinny little oven and I wouldn't mind it had been me," one of them said. "I never knew this Howard Johnson's was X-rated," the other one said. He held up one of the cans as if to offer it to Charlotte and the other one laughed. Charlotte felt old and awkward and dimly humiliated, a woman almost forty with a body that masqueraded as that of a young girl, a caricature of what they believed her to be. When she went back to the room Warren had the air-conditioning off and the windows closed and all the blankets and spreads from both beds piled over him. By Meridian he was having sweats and chills every day as he slept. By Meridian he did not sleep at night. By Meridian Howard Hollerith's girl was no longer with them. Charlotte supposed there had been a fight somewhere but she did not particularly remember it.

"I can't get it up," Warren said when she tried to wake him. "Baby, baby, I can't get it up."

"I don't want it," she said. "That's not what I want."

"Don't leave me. Don't leave me again."

"How could I leave you. Don't wake up."

How could I leave you.

The same way you left everybody.

"You like it too much," Warren said. "You like it more than anybody I ever knew. I know a girl in Birmingham likes it almost as much as you. We'll go do it with her. I want to see you with Julia."

"I didn't like that before."

"Did we do that before?"

"With Howard's girl. I didn't like it."

"You liked it all right."

We could have been doing this all our lives.

We should be doing this all our lives.

We should have done this all our lives, we should do this all our lives.

Talk about it and you lose it.

She was a woman almost forty whose fillings hurt when the highway vibrated. She was a woman almost forty waiting for the night she would call to get the Demerol. When Warren woke at sundown he took her to see a bike movie in a drive-in and drank a fifth of bourbon in the car and drove under the big pink arc lights with the rented car flat-out all the way to Birmingham. When the peonies swelled and broke behind her eyelids in the Ochsner Clinic they blazed like the big pink arc lights all the way to Birmingham. She could take care of somebody or somebody could take care of her and it was the same thing in the end.

Mérida.

Antigua.

Guadeloupe.

How could I leave you.

The same way you left everybody.

He wants you to walk away from here the same way you walked away from everything else in your life.

Tell her I said it's all the same.

El Aeropuerto del Presidente General Luis Strasser-Mendana, deceased.

Tell her that for me.

192

FIVE

OIL WELLS ABOUT TO COME IN HAVE A SOUND THE
attentive ear can detect.

As do earthquakes.

Volcanoes about to erupt transmit for days or weeks
before their convulsion a signal called "the harmonic
tremor."

Similarly I know for months before the fact
when there is about to be a "transition" in Boca
Grande. There is the occasional talk on the Avenida
Centrale. Sentries with carbines appear on the roof of
the presidential palace. For reasons I have never understood the postal rates begin to fluctuate mysteriously. There is a mounting mania for construction, for
getting one's cut while the government lasts: dummy
corporations multiply, phantom payrolls metastasize.
No one has an office but everyone has a mail drop.
A game is underway, the "winner" being the player
who lands his marker in the Ministry of Defense, and
the play has certain ritual moves: whoever wants the
Ministry that year must first get the *guerrilleros* into the

game. The *guerrilleros* seem always to believe that they are playing on their own, but they are actually a diversion, a disruptive element placed on the board only to be "quelled" by "stronger leadership." Guns and money begin to reach the *guerrilleros* via the usual channels. Mimeographed communiqués begin to appear, and twenty people are detained for questioning. A few are reported as prison suicides and a few more reported in exile but months later, again mysteriously, the same twenty are detained for questioning.

A mounting giddiness about the proximity of the *guerrilleros* sets the social tone of the city: many tea dances are planned, many adulterous liaisons initiated.

Many citizens adopt eccentric schedules to comply with the terms of their kidnapping insurance.

El Presidente, whoever is playing *El Presidente* at the moment, falls ill, and is urged to convalesce at Bariloche, in Argentina.

Gerardo arrives, and stays for the action.

These events in Boca Grande are inflexibly reported on the outside as signs of a popular uprising, but they are not. "NEW LEASE ON DEMOCRACY IN BOCA GRANDE" is one headline I recall from the *New York Times.* I believe Victor was the lessor of democracy in question.

I told Charlotte all along that I was hearing the harmonic tremor but Charlotte paid no attention.

Charlotte appeared to have used up all her attention.

2

I THINK NOW THAT IN THE BEGINNING SHE STAYED on in Boca Grande precisely because it seemed not to demand attentiveness. I recall having made, in the early days of my marriage to Edgar, somewhat the same mistake about Boca Grande, as well as about Edgar himself, but I revised my impressions to coincide with reality. Charlotte did the reverse. The city must have seemed to her at once familiar and distant, potentially "colorful" but in no way unmanageable, a place not unlike the matchbox model village that she and Dickie had once laid out along an irrigation ditch on the Hollister ranch: a place she could revise to suit herself as she had not been able to revise the other points on her recent itinerary. Here in Boca Grande there was the matchbox hotel in which one stayed, there was the matchbox hotel in which one did not stay. There was the "best" restaurant, there was the "second-best" restaurant, there were the districts in which nurses pushed baby carriages on Sunday afternoons and the districts in which nurses did not push baby carriages on Sunday afternoons.

There was no intimidating social life but only the Jockey Club, a place where a *norteamericana* in a good linen dress might well have expected to pass unnoticed.

There was no intimidating history but only the Museo de la República, a place where a *norteamericana* with a six-hundred-dollar handbag might well have expected to spend an undemanding hour studying cracked spinets and bronzed Winged Victories and other Strasser-Mendana family artifacts.

There were what seemed to Charlotte the "enchanting" children selling contraband Marlboro cigarettes outside the Caribe and there was what seemed to Charlotte the "amusing" accordionist playing "You're the Cream in My Coffee" in the Caribe lobby on Saturday nights and there were what must have seemed to Charlotte the toy soldiers with their toy carbines on the roof of the matchbox palace. The night Victor met Charlotte at the American Embassy Christmas party and took her for the first time to his apartment in the Residencia Vista del Palacio, Charlotte pulled back the curtains, gazed down at the palace, and pronounced its roof "ideal" for the fireworks which would officially open the mirage she was already calling the "Boca Grande Festival de Cine, First Annual." By the time Charlotte left Victor's apartment that night her festival was not only the First Annual but *Internacional*.

A few things about Boca Grande Charlotte did not perceive as toy.

She saw the American Embassy as "real" and she left her calling cards there in little lined envelopes embossed "Tiffany et Cie" and she never noticed the workmen who every morning scrubbed obscenities from the white limestone walls.

She saw the proximity of Caracas as "real" and she looked at a map every day to reassure herself on this point and she never knew that the four-lane Carretera del Libertador to Venezuela, marked so clearly on the maps, existed only on the maps, and possibly in the memory of whoever diverted the Alianza funding for the Carretera into the construction of the Residencia Vista del Palacio.

I believe this was Victor but it may have been Antonio.

It was certainly not Luis.

Luis was the Libertador to have been memorialized.

It occurs to me now that it could even have been Edgar but there remain some areas in which I, like Charlotte, prefer my own version.

As a matter of fact Charlotte saw everything about the actual geographical location of Boca Grande as "real," and crucial to her: in a certain dim way Charlotte believed that she had located herself at the very cervix of the world, the place through which a child lost to history must eventually pass. That Marin would turn up in Boca Grande Charlotte did not literally believe but never really doubted, at least until that day in September when Leonard told her where Marin actually was. Until that day when she learned for certain that Marin was not a victim of circumstance Charlotte believed without ever thinking it that she would be sitting at the Jockey Club one night and the waiter would tell her that a light-haired child who resembled her had come to the kitchen, applied for work as a waitness. Until that day when she learned for certain that Marin was not looking for her Charlotte believed instinctively that she would be buying the *Miami Herald* at the airport one morning and would hear a voice like her own on the tarmac.

Charlotte and Marin would share a room, order hot chocolate from room service, sit on the bed and catch up.

Charlotte and Marin would buy Marin a dress, get Marin a manicure, cure Marin's nerves with consommé and naps.

And when Marin was herself again Charlotte and Marin would drive to Caracas on the four-lane Carretera del Libertador, Charlotte and Marin would fly to Bogotá, Charlotte would show her only child the Andes.

Her only child.

Her oldest child.

The only child she ever dressed in flowered lawn for Easter.

One more thing in Boca Grande Charlotte saw as "real": the airport.

Of course the airport.

Perhaps because Charlotte believed in the airport and in the American Embassy and in the four-lane Carretera del Libertador to Venezuela she did not at first experience the weightless isolation which afflicts most visitors to Boca Grande. Perhaps because in those early days Charlotte had no letters to send or receive she did not notice that mail service was increasingly sporadic, that mailboxes all over the city were left to overflow and there was developing a currency market in stamps. Perhaps because for a while Charlotte had no calls to make or get she did not notice that the telephone lines were down more and more of the time, that calls to Miami were being routed through Quito and the American Embassy was resorting to ham radio to make routine contact with its consulate in Millonario.

She noticed that the lights at the Capilla del Mar resembled those at the Tivoli Gardens.

She did not notice that the pits in the porch railing at the Capilla del Mar resembled those made by carbine fire.

"Actually it doesn't involve me in the least," Charlotte told me. "I mean does it."

When I told Charlotte in March that there would come a day when it might be possible to interpret her presence in certain situations as "political."

"Actually I'm not 'political' in the least," Charlotte told me. "I mean my mind doesn't run that way."

When I told Charlotte in April that there would come a day when she should leave Boca Grande.

Meanwhile Charlotte would wait for Marin in this miniature capital where nothing need be real. Charlotte would remain as she waited an interested observer of everything she saw. Charlotte would remain a tourist, a traveler with good will and good credentials and no memory of how bougainvillea grew on a hotel wall in Mérida or how peonies could swell in a hospital room in New Orleans. Had Gerardo never come home Charlotte might have managed to maintain this fiction, although increasingly I doubt it.

Perhaps Gerardo does not play the motive role in this narrative I thought he did.

Perhaps only Charlotte Douglas and her husbands do.

Perhaps only Charlotte Douglas does, since it was Charlotte who chose to stay.

"YOU SMELL AMERICAN," WAS THE FIRST THING Gerardo ever said to Charlotte Douglas.

"I wonder if that could be because she *is*," Elena said.

"I wonder if *I* do," Ardis Bradley said.

I cannot now think how I happened to invite Charlotte for drinks that afternoon. It was Gerardo's second day home and he had asked to see only the family, and Tuck and Ardis Bradley, and Carmen Arrellano, who had been cultivating Antonio since Gerardo's last visit and on this particular afternoon was sulking in a hammock and ignoring her cousin, who happened to be passing the shrimp. As far as that went the only person Carmen Arrellano had acknowledged all afternoon was Antonio, and she had not exactly spoken to him. She had merely arched her back

slightly whenever he passed the hammock where she
lay.

But Charlotte.

I was not yet that close to Charlotte.

She had arrived in Boca Grande in November,
Victor and I had met her at the Embassy in December,
and when Gerardo came home it was late January,
early February. I had not yet seen the pictures in
Vogue of the last night she spent with her second
husband. I had not yet met her first in New Orleans. I
was just beginning cobalt, and was quite often tired,
and impatient, and generally more absorbed with some
gram-negative bacteria I was studying than with this
woman I did not understand.

I suppose I might have invited Charlotte only to
discomfit Victor.

Victor flatters himself that any woman he touches
is rendered unfit for normal social encounter.

In fact I have no idea why I invited Charlotte.

I only remember Charlotte arriving late and the sun
just falling and Gerardo watching her as she walked
across the lawn with the light behind her. I remember
her dress, a thin batiste dress with pale wildflowers
to her ankles. I remember her high-heeled sandals. I
remember thinking that she looked at once absurdly
frivolous and mildly "tragic," a word I do not use easily
or with any great approval.

"Look at her *bébé* dress," Elena said. Elena was
watching Gerardo. "Not that she is a *bébé*."

"So original actually," Ardis Bradley said. "If you
like that."

But Gerardo only watched Charlotte Douglas.

I remember that the grass was wet and that Charlotte walked very slowly and that when she stumbled
once on a sprinkler head she stopped and took off the

high-heeled sandals and then walked on toward us, barefoot.

"Very *déjeuner sur l'herbe*," Elena said.

"California," Ardis Bradley said.

I remember that Charlotte only kissed me absently and dropped into a wicker chair and did not speak.

You smell American.

I wonder if that could be because she *is*.

I wonder if *I* do.

And still Charlotte said nothing at all.

"You haven't met my son," I remember saying in the silence. "Gerardo. Mrs. Douglas. Mrs. Douglas is staying at the Caribe."

But Gerardo said nothing, only touched Charlotte's hair, a touch so tentative that it was almost not a touch at all.

Almost not a touch.

But it was.

"Extraordinary," Elena said.

"I wonder what 'American' smells like exactly," Ardis Bradley said.

Charlotte stood up then and without taking her eyes from Gerardo she brushed back her hair where he had touched it. She did not seem to know what to do with her hands after that and she fingered the batiste of her skirt. She looked unsteady, ill, stricken by some fever she did not understand, and when I put out my hand to steady her she flinched and pulled away.

"I don't like the Caribe," was the second thing Gerardo ever said to Charlotte Douglas.

His voice was low but so conversational and so unexceptional that for the moment after he spoke I could see Ardis Bradley marshaling opinions on the Caribe, pro and con.

Not Elena.

Elena's only developed instinct is for the presence of the sexual current.

"I want you to take an apartment," was the third thing Gerardo ever said to Charlotte Douglas.

4

Sexual current.

The retreat into pastoral imagery to suggest this current has always seemed to me curious and decadent.

The dissolve through the goldenrod.

The romance of the rose.

Equally specious.

As usual I favor a mechanical view.

What Charlotte and Gerardo did that afternoon was reverse the entire neutron field on my lawn, exhausting and disturbing and altering not only the mood but possibly the cell structure (I am interested in this possibility) of everyone there. Charlotte never spoke at all to Gerardo, only turned away and engaged Tuck Bradley in one of those reflective monologues she tended to initiate at the instant of distraction. It sometimes seemed to me that these monologues had for Charlotte the same protective function that ink has for a squid. This one touched on whether or not Tuck Bradley had ever been in the courtroom when Leonard did "one of his really dazzling redirects" (Tuck Brad-

206

ley had not); what Tuck Bradley thought about the national lottery (Tuck Bradley saw both its "good points" and its "bad points"); what Tuck Bradley thought about assassination in the United States (Tuck Bradley thought it "deplorable"); and what "offbeat" hotels Tuck Bradley could recommend in Paris.

Tuck Bradley recommended the George V.

"What about London," Charlotte said, her voice suddenly weary. She did not turn to meet Gerardo's gaze.

"I would say . . ." Tuck Bradley tamped his pipe. "The Savoy."

Charlotte took a drink from a tray and I wanted to see what she would do with it. Charlotte never exactly "drank" a drink. Sometimes she drained it like a child and sometimes she just played with the ice and quite often she dropped it. This time she set it on a tiled bench, quite carefully, without tasting it.

"Or Claridge's," Tuck Bradley said.

There was a silence.

"I want to jot all this down," Charlotte said vaguely, and then she turned away from Tuck Bradley.

Gerardo watched her as she ran across the lawn.

Victor watched her as she ran across the lawn.

Antonio crouched on the lawn by Carmen Arrellano's hammock and watched Gerardo and Victor.

"This is so absorbing but you can take me home now," Carmen Arrellano said to Antonio.

"*Norteamericana* cunt," Antonio said without moving.

"And I suppose another choice in Paris would be . . ." Tuck Bradley was still intent on his pipe. "The Plaza Athénée."

"She'll definitely want to jot that down," Elena said. "Possibly you could catch her and tell her. The Plaza

Athénée. Are we going to get dinner? Is anyone going to *le* Jockey?"

"Did Charlotte Douglas say she was going to Paris?" Ardis Bradley said.

" '*Le* Jockey,' " Carmen Arrellano said to Antonio. "Listen to Elena. Your interesting sister-in-law thinks she's in Paris. I don't want dinner."

"I mean if she *is* going to Paris," Ardis Bradley said, "she's going to miss her husband."

I looked at Ardis Bradley.

She could not have had more than two drinks but she did not drink well.

No one else seemed to have heard what she said.

"*I* want dinner," Elena said. "And I also want to go to Paris."

"Go to Paris." Antonio rose from his crouch. Some chemical exchange in his brain seemed to have switched on another of his rages. I used to be interested in Antonio's cell metabolism. "Go to Paris, go to Geneva. Buy a parrot. Buy two parrots, give one to your friend the *norteamericana* cunt."

"The *norteamericana* cunt is not your sister-in-law's friend," Carmen Arrellano murmured from the depths of the hammock. "The *norteamericana* cunt is Victor's friend."

"Gerardo will drop you home now, Carmen." Victor spoke very clearly in a tired voice. His eyes were closed. "Won't you. Gerardo."

"No," Antonio said. "He won't."

"Antonio is going to drop Carmen home," Gerardo said. He was still gazing across the lawn. "Antonio is either going to drop Carmen home or Antonio is going to drop Carmen in Arizona. With Isabel and Dr. Schiff. Carmen's choice. Why is she here?"

"Who?" Victor said.

"Mrs. Douglas."

"More to the point, why are you here?" Victor did not open his eyes. "Why aren't you off bobsledding somewhere."

"I thought my country needed me," Gerardo said. He did not turn around. *"Patria,* Victor. Right or wrong. Where exactly is Mr. Douglas?"

The only sound was that of the DDT truck which grinds past this house early each evening to spray.

"Caracas," Ardis Bradley said.

This time everyone seemed to have heard what Ardis Bradley said.

"Or he was when he called Tuck."

Victor opened his eyes and stared at her.

"Wasn't it Caracas? Tuck?"

"I have no idea." Tuck Bradley stood up. "It's time, Ardis."

"I have always loathed that phrase. 'It's time, Ardis.' You told me Caracas."

"We'll get dinner, Ardis."

Ardis Bradley stood up unsteadily.

I watched the cloud of DDT settle over the spindly roses at the far end of the lawn.

It occurred to me that my attempt to grow roses and a lawn at the equator was a delusion worthy of Charlotte Douglas.

One of whose husbands appeared to be in Caracas.

Not a delusion at all.

"Is he coming here?" Victor said suddenly.

"I would rather hope not," Tuck Bradley said, and he smiled, and he took Ardis Bradley's arm and after they left no one spoke for a long time. I think no one bothered to get dinner that night except Charlotte, who was seen at the Jockey Club as usual and was reported to have eaten not only the *plato frío* and the spiny lobster but two orders of flan.

At the time this surprised me.

At the time I had no real idea of how oblivious Charlotte Douglas was to the disturbance she could cause in the neutron field of a room, or a lawn.

5

As a matter of fact Leonard Douglas did not come to Boca Grande that spring.

Leonard Douglas did not come to Boca Grande until early September, at a time when the airport was closed at least part of every day while the carriers negotiated with the *guerrilleros* and when visitors to the Caribe were routinely frisked before they could enter the dining room.

I have no idea whether he had even intended to come in the spring, or what he had called Tuck Bradley to say.

Or to ask.

Neither Ardis nor Tuck Bradley ever mentioned the call from Caracas again.

If he had called from Caracas to ask about Charlotte he never took the next step and called Charlotte herself: Victor had her calls monitored, both at the Caribe and at the apartment on the Avenida del Mar she rented the week after she met Gerardo, and, at least until the week the *guerrilleros* knocked out the central monitoring system, there was no record of a call from Leonard Douglas to Charlotte Douglas.

Nor, on the other hand, was there any record of a call from Leonard Douglas to Tuck Bradley, which made Victor depressed and suspicious about his Embassy surveillance team.

I believe he put the entire team under what he called "internal surveillance," but it turned out to be just another case of mechanical failure.

Most things at the Ministry did.

I recall thinking that Victor would not be entirely sorry to turn over the Ministry to whoever was trying to get it that year.

"You're aware Gerardo's still seeing the *norteamericana,*" Victor said one morning in March.

I knew that he was disturbed because he had come to see me in my laboratory. Victor does not like to see me in my laboratory. His forehead sweats, his pupils contract. I have observed taboo systems in enough cultures to know precisely how Victor feels about me in my laboratory: Victor distrusts the scientific method, and my familiarity with it gives me a certain power over him.

In my laboratory I am therefore particularly taboo.

To Victor.

For some years I used this taboo to my advantage but I am no longer so sure that Victor was not right.

"I believe they're 'dating,' Victor." I did not look up from what I was doing. "I see her too. What about it."

"I'm not talking about you seeing her."

"I took her to Millonario. She killed a chicken. With her bare hands."

"I'm not talking about you seeing her and I'm not

212

talking about any chickens seeing her. I'm talking about Gerardo seeing her. Observed at all hours. Entering and leaving. I don't like it."

"Why don't you have him deported," I said.

Victor took another tack.

"You're very sophisticated these days."

I said nothing.

"Very tolerant."

I said nothing.

"I suppose with your vast sophistication and tolerance you don't mind the fact that your son *also* spends time with the faggot. The West Indian faggot. Whatever his circus name is, I'm not familiar with it."

I transferred a piece of tissue from one solution to another.

Victor meant Bebe Chicago.

Victor was as familiar with Bebe Chicago's name as I was, probably more familiar, since Victor received a detailed report on Bebe Chicago every morning at nine o'clock.

With his coffee.

"I sometimes wonder if your son has leanings. That way."

"No need to worry about the *norteamericana,* then."

Victor drummed his fingers on a flask and watched me for a long time without speaking.

"The West Indian is financing the *guerrilleros,*" he said suddenly. "I happen to know that."

"I know you 'happen to know that,' Victor. You told me a year ago. When Gerardo and Elena were such a burden to you."

"It doesn't make any difference to you that this West Indian is financing the *guerrilleros?*"

"It doesn't make any difference to you either. If it did you'd arrest him."

213

"I don't arrest him because I don't want to embarrass your son."

I said nothing.

Victor would have arrested me if he thought he could carry it off.

"All right then," Victor said. "You tell me why I don't arrest him."

"You don't arrest him because you want to know who's financing *him*. That's why you don't arrest him."

Victor sat in silence drumming his fingers on the flask.

It was the usual unsolved equation of the harmonic tremor in Boca Grande.

If Bebe Chicago was running the *guerrilleros* then X must be running Bebe Chicago.

Who was X.

This time.

There you had it. The *guerrilleros* would stage their "expropriations" and leave their communiqués about the "People's Revolution" and everyone would know who was financing the *guerrilleros* but for a while no one would know for whose benefit the *guerrilleros* were being financed. In the end the *guerrilleros* would all be shot and the true players would be revealed.

Mirabile dictu.

People we knew.

I remembered Luis using the *guerrilleros* against Anastasio Mendana-Lopez and I also remember Victor using the *guerrilleros*, against Luis.

I only think that.

I never knew that. Empirically.

In this case of course it would turn out to be Antonio who was using the *guerrilleros*, against Victor, but no one understood this in March.

Except Gerardo.

Gerardo understood it in March.

Maybe Carmen Arrellano understood it in March too.

Charlotte never did understand it.

I don't know that either. Empirically.

"I suppose you *do* know who's running the West Indian?" Victor said after a while. He was still drumming his fingers on the flask, a barrage of little taps, a tattoo. "I suppose in your infinite wisdom you know who's running the West Indian and one day you might deign to tell me?"

"How would I know who's running the West Indian, Victor? I'm not the Minister of Defense. You might want to watch that flask you're banging around, it's cancer virus." It was not cancer virus but I liked to reinforce the taboo. "Live."

Victor stood up abruptly.

"Disgusting," he said finally. "Filthy. Crude. The thought of it makes me retch."

"Are you talking about the cancer virus or the *guerrilleros?*"

"I am talking," he whispered, his voice strangled, "about the kind of woman who would kill a chicken with her bare hands."

It occurred to me that morning that Charlotte Douglas was acquiring certain properties of taboo.

Which might have stood her in good stead.

Had Victor been in charge at the Estadio Nacional instead of waiting it out with *El Presidente* at Bariloche.

6

WHEN MARIN BOGART ASKED ME WITHOUT MUCH interest what her mother had "done" in Boca Grande there was very little I could think to say.

Very little that Marin Bogart would have understood.

A lost child in a dirty room in Buffalo.

A child who claimed no interest in the past.

Or the future.

Or the present.

As far as I could see.

"She did some work in a clinic," I said.

"Charity," Marin Bogart said.

The indictment lay between us for a while.

"Cholera actually," I said.

Marin Bogart shrugged.

Cholera was something Marin Bogart had been protected against, along with diphtheria, pertussis, tetanus, tuberculosis, poliomyelitis, and undue dental decay.

Cholera was one more word Marin Bogart did not understand.

"And after that she worked in a birth control clinic."

"Classic," Marin Bogart said. "Absolutely classic."

"How exactly is it 'classic.' "

"Birth control is *the* most flagrant example of how the ruling class practices genocide."

"Maybe not *the* most flagrant," I said.

A lost daughter in a dirty room in Buffalo with dishes in the sink and an M–3 on the bed.

A daughter who never had much use for words but had finally learned to string them together so that they sounded almost like sentences.

A daughter who chose to believe that her mother had died on the wrong side of a "people's revolution."

"There was no 'right side,' " I said. "There was no issue. There were only—"

"That is a typically—"

"There were only personalities."

"—*A typically bourgeois view of the revolutionary process.*"

She had Charlotte's eyes.

Maybe there is no motive role in this narrative.

Maybe it is just something that happened.

Then why is it in my mind when nothing else is.

7

WHAT HAD CHARLOTTE DOUGLAS "DONE" IN BOCA Grande.

I have no idea whether Marin Bogart was asking me that day what her mother had "done" with her life in Boca Grande or what her mother had "done" to get killed in Boca Grande.

In either case the answer is obscure.

The question of Charlotte Douglas has never been "settled" for me.

Never "decided."

I know how to make models of life itself, DNA, RNA, helices double and single and squared, but I try to make a model of Charlotte Douglas's "character" and I see only a shimmer.

Like the shimmer of the oil slick on the boulevards after rain in Progreso.

Let me try a less holistic approach to the model.

We had the cholera epidemic in April that year.

The cholera epidemic in which Charlotte volunteered

218

to give inoculations, and did, for thirty-four hours without sleeping.

I gave inoculations with Charlotte, but only for a few hours the first morning, because I had no patience with the fact that almost no one in Boca Grande would cross the street to be inoculated. They were all *fatalistas* about cholera. Cholera was an opportunity for God to prove His love.

"Then let Him prove it," I said to Charlotte at the end of the first morning.

"We have to make it attractive," Charlotte said. "Obviously."

And she did.

She set out to make each inoculation seem to the inoculee not a hedge against the hereafter but an occasion of mild profit in the here and now. She left the clinic for an hour and she bought chocolates wrapped in pink tinfoil from the Caribe kitchen and she made a deal for whisky miniatures with an unemployed Braniff steward who had access to the airport catering trucks and, until the remaining vaccine was appropriated by a colonel named Rafael Higuera, she dispensed these favors with every 1.5 cc. shot of Lederle Cholera Strains Ogawa-Inaba.

"Why didn't she just lie down and open her legs for them," Antonio said to Gerardo in my living room. It was the evening of the day the vaccine had been appropriated and Antonio had already expressed his conviction that Higuera had performed a public service by preventing Charlotte from further contaminating the populace with her American vaccine. I have never known why Antonio was so particularly enraged by everything Charlotte did. I suppose she was a *norteamericana*, she was a woman, she was an unpredictable element. I suppose she was a version of me at whom he could vent his rage. "Ask the great lady why she didn't just do that. Higuera didn't go far *enough*."

"How far should he have gone," Gerardo said, and smiled slightly at me.

"She'd throw her apron on my feet once," Antonio said. "Just once."

"What would you do," Gerardo said.

"Drop her," Antonio said.

"Drop her," Gerardo said.

"Between the eyes."

"Seems extreme," Gerardo said.

"How can you be entertained by this?" I said to Gerardo.

"How can you not be?" Gerardo said to me.

During the week after the appropriation of the vaccine Charlotte spoke not at all to me, spoke only in a glazed and distracted way to Gerardo, and was known to have placed two telephone calls to Leonard Douglas, neither of them completed. At the end of the week she gave me her revised version of the appropriation of the vaccine, the version in which the army was lending its resources to the inoculation program, the version in which she had simply misunderstood Higuera, the version in which he had never offered to sell her the vaccine but had simply expressed concern as to whether she herself had been inoculated; once she had arrived at this version Charlotte never mentioned cholera again, although people continued dying from it for several weeks.

After the cholera epidemic she appeared for a while that May and June to retreat into unspecified gastro-intestinal infection less often, and she perfected that frenetic public energy which made many people, particularly Elena, suspect her of a reliance on major

amphetamines. Even after she had moved most of her
things into the apartment on the Avenida del Mar, even
after she had with her own hands whitewashed all the
walls and filled the empty rooms with flowers and
begun to have what she called her "evenings" there,
she kept her room at the Caribe, and she would go
there every day for breakfast and to spend most of
the day.

She began her "writing" during these days she spent
alone at the Caribe.

She remembered her "film festival," and she drew
up endless lists of names: actors, directors, agents,
former agents who were then studio executives, former
studio executives who were then independent pro-
ducers, and what I once heard her call "other movers
and shakers." She had met many of these people with
Leonard and she was certain that they would be de-
lighted to lend their names and films, once she put it
to them.

Which she intended to do as soon as she completed
the lists.

She got the idea for her "boutique," and she planned
her projected inventory: needlepoint canvases of her
own design and Porthault linens, the market for which
in Boca Grande would have seemed to be limited to
Elena, Bianca, Isabel, and me. She had enlisted Gerardo's help in finding a storefront to rent and she was
certain that the boutique would pick up the character
of the entire neighborhood, once she got it in shape
for the opening.

Which she intended to do as soon as Bebe Chicago
got his Dominicans out of the storefront.

"Imagine cymbidiums," she said on the afternoon
she showed me her storefront. "Masses of them. In

hemp baskets. The illusion of the tropics. That's the effect to strive for."

As a matter of fact the illusion of the tropics seemed to me an odd effect to strive for in a city rotting on the equator, but the actual condition of the storefront was such that I could only nod. The room was cramped and grimy and the single window was blacked out. Outside the afternoon sun was blazing but inside there was only the light from two bare bulbs. In the room, besides Charlotte and me, there were several sleeping bags, a hot plate, an open and unflushed toilet, a cheap dinette chair in which Bebe Chicago sat talking on the telephone, and a table at which a man whom Charlotte had introduced as "Mr. Sanchez" seemed to be translating a United States Army arms manual into Spanish.

Charlotte appeared oblivious.

"Lighten, brighten, open it up. The perfect creamy white on the walls, maybe the *palest* robin's-egg on the ceiling. And lattice. Lots of lattice. Mr. Sanchez is doing the lattice for me." Charlotte smiled fondly at the man at the table. He did not smile back. "Aren't you."

"Mr. Sanchez" stared at Charlotte as if she were a moth he had never before observed and turned to Bebe Chicago. "Are we interested in the AR-16?" he said in Spanish.

"AR-15 only." Bebe Chicago hung up the telephone and smiled at me. "Gerardo's mama naturally speaks Spanish, *mon chéri*."

"Think of a lath-house crossed with a Givenchy perfume box," Charlotte said.

"Can I offer Gerardo's mama a *café-filtre*," Bebe Chicago said. He stood up with a magician's flourish and placed the dinette chair in front of me. "Can I

222

offer Gerardo's mama this superb example of post-industrial craftsmanship."

I remained standing.

"Possibly gardenias," Charlotte said. "No. Cymbidiums."

Bebe Chicago smiled and sat in the chair himself.

"Then can I tell Gerardo's mama how much I admire her shoes," he said. "Can I at least tell her that."

"You can tell her what that Bren gun is doing behind the toilet," I said.

"That's not a Bren at all," Bebe Chicago said after only the slightest beat, his voice still silky. "That's a Kalashnikov. Russian. Out of Syria. The Chinese make one too, but it's inferior to the Russian. The Russian is the best. A really super weapon."

"Don't talk about guns," Charlotte said, and her voice was low and abrupt, and after that day she seemed to lose interest in her boutique.

During this period Charlotte also had her "research."

She had her "paperwork."

In other words she would sit alone in her room at the Caribe and she would try to read books and she would try to write letters. She tried to read a book about illiteracy in Latin America, but in lieu of finishing it she wrote a letter to *Prensa Latina* offering her services as author of a daily "literacy lesson." She tried to read Alberto Masferrer's *El Mínimum Vital* but she still had difficulty reading Spanish, and she had read a hundred pages of *El Mínimum Vital* before she learned from Gerardo that it was about the progressive tax. She borrowed from Ardis Bradley a volume that was obviously a CIA-sponsored "handbook" on Boca Grande, and she discovered in the introduction to this handbook an invitation to address her suggestions "for factual or interpretive or other changes" to a post-office box in Washington.

To this post-office box in Washington Charlotte addressed her suggestions for factual or interpretive or other changes on the subject of Boca Grande.

She never received an answer but first Kasindorf and then Riley and finally Tuck Bradley received word that she was in the country.

In case they had missed her.

Nor did Charlotte receive answers from most of the other officials and agencies and writers and editors to whom she addressed her suggestions for factual or interpretive or other changes on a wide range of subjects.

I believe mainly "other" changes.

The only bad time of these days Charlotte spent at the Caribe was about four o'clock.

At about four o'clock the shine of plausibility would seem to go off her projects.

At about four o'clock she would find herself sitting in the room at the Caribe remembering something.

She would sometimes call me up at four o'clock and tell me what she was remembering.

For example.

Those crossed spots on the Pollock in the dining room of the house on California Street.

Those crossed spots were too bright, or too exposed, she could not determine which.

Those spots had always been too bright, too exposed.

She should perhaps have them recessed in the ceiling.

What did I think.

At a certain point during each of these calls the possession would seem to fade from her voice, and by the time she hung up she would sound almost at peace. She would go downstairs then and sit by the pool and she would watch the peacocks hiding from the heat under the jacaranda trees and she would watch the blocks of ice being dragged across the concrete into the Caribe kitchen. She would imagine the various bacteria waiting in each block of ice. She counted bacteria instead of sheep. After a while a great lassitude would come over her and she would want to sleep, and sometimes she did sleep, there by the Caribe pool in the late afternoons, but at night in the apartment on the Avenida del Mar she did not sleep at all.

8

WE COULD HAVE BEEN DOING THIS ALL OUR LIVES.
We should do this all our lives.
Tell her I said it's all the same.
Tell her that for me.
Tell Charlotte she was wrong.
I never told Charlotte what Warren Bogart said.
I think she heard him say it every night.

She would get up some nights when Gerardo was
asleep and she would pick up the half-filled glasses
with which the strangers who came to her "evenings"
had littered the empty rooms of the apartment on the
Avenida del Mar and she would walk by herself to a
theater downtown which showed dolorous Mexican
movies all night, tales of betrayal and stolen babies
and other sexual punishments. Other nights she would
not leave the apartment but would only stand in the
living room by the window and listen to the radio.
Radio Boca Grande was allowed to broadcast only
during restricted hours by that time but she could
usually get Radio Jamaica and sometimes even Radio

226

British Honduras and the Voice of the Caribbean from the Central American Mission in San José, Costa Rica. She thought she had New Orleans or Miami one night, dance music from some hotel or another in New Orleans or Miami, but it turned out to be only a pick-up from the Caribe. She recognized the accordionist.

Some nights when she could not even get Radio Jamaica she called San Francisco.

She did not call the number of the house on California Street in San Francisco.

She did not call the number of anyone she knew in San Francisco.

She called a number in San Francisco which gave, over and over again in a voice so monotonous as to seem to come from beyond the grave, the taped "road condition" report of the California Highway Patrol.

Interstate 80 Donner Pass was open.

U.S. 50 Echo Summit was closed.

State Route 88 Carson Pass was open.

State Route 89 Lassen Loop was closed, State Route 108 Sonora was closed, State Route 120 Tioga Pass was closed.

These calls were routed through Quito and Miami and took quite a long time to place.

By the end of May every road regularly reported upon by the California Highway Patrol was open.

According to Victor.

Who duly heard these calls and believed them coded.

"Quite frankly I don't think the California Highway Patrol is hooked up with the *guerrilleros*," I said to Victor.

"Then give me one reason for these calls."

"She's lonely, Victor." In fact "lonely" was never a word I would have used to characterize Charlotte

Douglas but conversation with Victor requires broad strokes. "She's 'a woman alone.' As I believe you used to call her."

"She is no longer a woman alone. May I point out. On the occasion of all but one of these calls your son has been spending the night in this apartment. Where Bebe Chicago has been a frequent visitor."

"If I were you I'd listen to Bebe Chicago's calls and forget Charlotte's."

"Bebe Chicago's calls. Spare me any more of Bebe Chicago's calls." Victor mimicked a whispery falsetto. " 'Ricardo? It's me. *C'est moi, chéri.* Bebe.' "

"Actually you aren't good at voices, Victor. What is it you want to know?"

"What I want to know, Grace, is what your son is doing while she makes these calls."

"Sleeping."

" 'Sleeping'?"

" 'Sleeping.' Yes."

Victor looked at me awhile, and then at his nails.

"Sleeping," he said finally. "What kind of man would be sleeping."

I was tired of Victor that spring.

I was also tired of whatever game Gerardo was playing with Bebe Chicago and the *guerrilleros* and the strangers he invited to Charlotte's "evenings" on the Avenida del Mar.

Charlotte's "evenings."

I would go sometimes.

There were always these strangers there, third-rate people Gerardo was using in his game, the object of which seemed to be to place his marker in Victor's office in as few moves as possible. His marker that year happened to be Antonio, but who it was mattered not at all to Gerardo. Gerardo plays only for the action. Part of the action in this case was the artful manipulation of what passed for the intelligentsia in Boca Grande, the point being to create an illusion of support for the *guerrilleros,* and it was the members of this "intelligentsia" who littered the apartment on the Avenida del Mar with half-filled glasses two or three nights a week. Of course Bebe Chicago was usually there, and a few "poets" who had published verses in anthologies with titles like *Fresh Wind in the Caribbean,* and the usual complement of translators and teachers and film critics who supported themselves stringing for newspapers and playing at politics. I recall one who read out loud at Charlotte's dinner table a paper he was writing called "The Singular Position of Intellectuals with Respect to the Crisis of the Underdeveloped World" and then read it again, over Charlotte's telephone, to a friend in Tenerife. I recall another who made marionettes to perform the plays of Arnold Wesker in schoolyards.

I have no idea what Charlotte thought of these people.

She told me she found them "terribly stimulating to listen to," but I never saw her "listen to" any one of them.

She had in the dining room of the apartment on the Avenida del Mar a large round table around which these people sat and talked about what they always called "the truly existential situation of the Central American," and Charlotte would sit at this table in her gray chiffon dress, but she seemed not to be there at all. She only stared at the kerosene lamp in the center of the table and watched moths batter themselves against the glass chimney. As the moths fell stunned to the table she would brush them toward her with a napkin, like someone dreaming. At the end of such an evening there would be moths drifted beneath her chair and moth wings caught in her gray chiffon skirt and no trace in her mind of what had been said. So dimly did Charlotte appear to perceive the nature of her evenings that she would sometimes invite Victor, and Victor would sit stiffly and finger his pistol and say that he did not quite comprehend why the situation of the Central American was so truly existential.

"What's to be done about it in any case," I recall Victor saying one night. "What does it mean."

Whenever I saw Victor at one of Charlotte's "evenings" I found myself rather liking him.

At least he was serious.

Unlike Gerardo.

"Don't worry about what it means," Gerardo said that night.

"'What does it mean,'" Bebe Chicago said. "A knotty question."

"I find it touching," the most offensive of the poets said. His name was Raúl Lara and he was working on a sequence of Mother-and-Child sonnets to present to the people of Cuba and all that evening he had been studying a mango, spitting on it, polishing it, holding it in different lights.

Raúl Lara held the mango now in front of Victor's eyes.

"A Strasser-Mendana. A man of action. Trapped in the quicksand of time and he asks us *what does it mean*. Give him Fanon. Give him Debray. Give him this fat mango."

Raúl Lara dropped the mango in Victor's lap.

With considerable dignity Victor stood up and placed the mango on the table in front of Charlotte.

The table fell silent.

Charlotte seemed to force herself to look away from the moths and at the mango. "Did someone need a fruit knife," she said finally.

"You weren't listening," Victor said gently.

"She never listens," Gerardo said.

"Why don't you listen," Victor said to Charlotte.

Charlotte smiled vaguely.

"Maybe she doesn't listen because she's afraid of what she'll hear," Raúl Lara said. "New ideas. Very threatening."

Charlotte looked directly at Raúl Lara for the first time that evening. She seemed tired. She seemed older. "I've heard some new ideas," she said after a while. "In my time."

Other than that Charlotte seemed to make no judgments at all on the people who came to the apartment on the Avenida del Mar, no judgments on them and no distinctions among them.

Among us.

I was there too.

We were voices. We were voices no different from the voices in Mexican movies. We were voices no different from the voices on Radio Jamaica or on the California Highway Patrol road reports. We were voices to fill the hours until it was time to go to the Caribe for breakfast.

Sometimes I forget that I was there too.

Charlotte's breakfasts at the Caribe.

Charlotte went to the Caribe for breakfast every morning for a while.

She went to the Caribe for breakfast because she

worried about three children who every morning would crawl under the Caribe fence and leap screaming into the deep end of the pool. They did not seem to know how to swim. They would flounder and gasp to the side and leap in again. There was no lifeguard and the water was green with algae and Charlotte could never see the children beneath the surface of the water but every morning she would take her breakfast to the pool and try to insure that the children did not drown. She tried to distinguish their particular shrieks. She counted their heads compulsively. Because she believed that in the instant of a blink one of the heads would slip beneath the surface and stay there unseen she tried not to blink.

"There are no children registered at the hotel," the manager of the Caribe said when she mentioned the children in the pool. "So they aren't supposed to be there."

"But they are there."

"They aren't supposed to be there," the manager said, enunciating each word very carefully, "because there are no children registered at the hotel."

On the morning she could only see two of the three children for thirty straight seconds she screamed, and jumped into the pool with her clothes on. She choked and the murky water blinded her and when she came up all three children were standing on the edge of the pool fighting over her handbag. She watched them run away with the bag and she went upstairs and she stood for a long while in the lukewarm trickle from the shower and she thought about the pale wash of green Marin got in her hair every summer from the chlorine in pools.

California pools.

Swimming pools for children who knew how to swim.

She tried to stop thinking about swimming pools but could not.

"You don't seem to have heard of chlorine here," she said to me.

"We don't want to emphasize technology at the expense of traditional culture," I said.

I thought she was in a less literal mood than usual but apparently she was not.

"I see," she said.

"I wasn't serious," I said. "It was a joke. Irony."

"Is cheap," she said. Her expression did not change.

After that morning at the pool she stopped spending her days at the Caribe and volunteered as an advisor at the birth control clinic. She seemed to have entirely forgotten Colonel Higuera and the Lederle cholera vaccine, her previous essay into good works. She was a source of some exasperation at the birth control clinic, because she kept advising the women to request diaphragms they would never use instead of intrauterine devices they could not remove, but the job of "advisor" was largely academic anyway since only intrauterine devices were available. In any case Charlotte took her work very seriously and it seemed to lend a purpose to her days.

"Anyone can learn to use a diaphragm," she announced at my house one evening when I suggested that the diaphragm, however favored it might be in the practices of San Francisco gynecologists, was not generally considered the most practical means of birth control in underdeveloped countries. "I certainly did."

"You certainly did what?" Gerardo said.

"I certainly learned to use a diaphragm."

"Of course you did," Gerardo said. "What's that got to do with it? Grace wasn't talking about you."

"Grace was talking," Charlotte said, "about the difficulty of using diaphragms. And I said there wasn't any. Difficulty. Because I had no trouble whatsoever learning how."

Gerardo looked at me.

I think this was perhaps Gerardo's first exposure not to the *norteamericana* in Charlotte but to the westerner in Charlotte, the Hollister ranch child in Charlotte, the strain in Charlotte which insisted that the world was peopled with others exactly like herself.

"What is she saying," Gerardo said to me.

"Charlotte is an egalitarian," I said to Gerardo. "So am I. You are not."

"I am only saying," Charlotte said patiently, "that if I could learn to use a diaphragm then anyone could."

"Bullshit," Gerardo said.

Charlotte looked at Gerardo levelly for quite a long time.

There was a flicker of Warren Bogart on her face.

"Then don't you talk at me any more about what 'the people' can do," she said finally.

No irony.

However cheap.

I liked Charlotte very much that night but she still tended to take whatever Gerardo said precisely at face value. Gerardo only talked about "the people" that spring as a move in the particular game he was playing. As a matter of fact Charlotte tended to take what anyone said precisely at face value. When she showed me her next attempt at writing about Boca Grande, the next of those "Letters from Central America" which were the only one of her projects to survive the incident at the Caribe pool, the typed manuscript began: "A nation that refuses to emphasize technology at the expense of its traditional culture, Boca Grande is . . ."

Boca Grande is.

9

"YOU SHOULDN'T HAVE DONE THAT," I SAID TO Victor the day Antonio's Bentley exploded in front of the Caribe, killing the chauffeur. Antonio had not even been using the Bentley. Carmen Arrellano had been using the Bentley, but at the instant of the explosion Carmen Arrellano had been having her legs waxed in the Caribe beauty shop. In short the job had been inept in the extreme, but this was not the aspect I wanted to stress with Victor. "You really shouldn't have."

"I didn't," Victor said. "I'm appalled you think I did. Appalled. Shocked. Hurt. It's an obscene accusation."

I said nothing.

"If you think I did it," Victor said after a while, "then you know why I did it. You're aware of what Antonio's trying to do."

I said nothing.

"I suppose your son told you," Victor said.

"Actually no."

"I suppose you prefer Antonio to me," Victor said.

"Not particularly."

Victor sat in silence for a while. He had come to visit in the middle of the afternoon. He never used to visit in the middle of the afternoon. Victor did not seem to know what to do with his afternoons that summer.

"Then why aren't you helping me," he said finally. "You know what Antonio's doing, you—"

"I don't know. I just suppose."

"—You *suppose* you know what Antonio's doing, why don't you discuss it with me? Why aren't you *with* me?"

"Because it doesn't make any difference to me," I said.

Victor sat slumped in a chair.

I have liked Victor on some occasions and pitied him on many. Edgar called him stupid. Luis laughed at him. Even Antonio was making a fool of him.

I took his ridiculous manicured hand.

"Because it's going to happen," I said. "Just let it happen. With grace."

"I can't do that," Victor said after a while.

I knew he couldn't do that.

Within the next two weeks three more explosions occurred in locations where Antonio might normally have been, killing six and injuring fourteen, and then there was the usual odd calm.

" 'The outlook is not all bright.' " Charlotte was reading me the draft of an unfinished "Letter from Central America." " 'Nor is the outlook all black.' Paragraph. 'Nonetheless—' "

She broke off.

"That's where I seem to be blocked."

"I don't wonder," I said.

"What do you mean."

" 'Nevertheless' *what?* I mean, Charlotte. If you say 'the outlook is not all bright' and then you say 'nor is the outlook all black,' then you can't start the next sentence with 'nevertheless.' It can't possibly mean anything."

"I didn't start the next sentence with 'nevertheless,' " I said nothing.

"Anyway." Charlotte folded the pages of her unfinished Letter with a neat vertical crease as children fold their weekly themes. "It's not just a new sentence. It's a new paragraph."

It occurred to me that I had never before had so graphic an illustration of how the consciousness of the human organism is carried in its grammar.

Or the unconsciousness of the human organism.

If the organism under scrutiny is Charlotte.

"In any case," Charlotte said after a while. "It'll all fall together when I'm away."

"You're going away, then."

"Of course I'm going away. I mean I don't live here, do I."

"When?"

"I'm not quite sure when."

"Where?"

"I have to see someone."

I did not ask who.

"Or rather I want to see someone. My husband."

I did not ask which one.

"But I mean there's no immediate rush about it. Is there."

"I think there is, Charlotte." I was suddenly tired. "As a matter of fact I think it's imperative that you go very soon."

"No." She seemed abruptly agitated. "It is not imperative. At all. *He is not dying.*"

I sat without speaking awhile.

The tissue around Charlotte's eyes was reddening but she did not cry.

Tell Charlotte she was wrong.

"I didn't mean that it's imperative you go anywhere in particular," I said finally. "I don't care where you go. Go to Caracas, go to Managua. Just get out of here."

She put on her dark glasses and tried to smile.

"Just leave," I said.

"I don't believe I can quite manage this display of hospitality." There was in Charlotte's voice an inflection of which she seemed entirely unaware, an inflection I had heard before only in the Garden District of New Orleans. "Here's-your-hat-what's-your hurry, seems about the size of it."

Here's-your-hat-what's-your-hurry.

Mrs. Fayard's been learning West Texas manners.

Tell Charlotte she was wrong.

"Charlotte." I felt as if I were talking to a child. "I've told you before, there is trouble here. There is going to be more trouble here. You are going to find yourself in the middle of this trouble which is not your business."

"I don't know anything about any trouble. So how could I possibly be in the middle of it."

"Because *Gerardo is.*"

She looked at me as if I had mentioned someone she had met a long time before and did not quite remember.

I think I fucked you one Easter.

I think I did that and forgot it.

I think she did forget it.

"In any case I'm not affected," she said after a while. "Because I'm simply not interested in any causes or issues."

"Neither is anyone here."

Charlotte said nothing.

"Charlotte," I tried again. "What do you think all those people were doing at your dining-room table?"

Charlotte looked at me.

"You were there too," she said finally.

That was July.

Boca Grande is.

10

I RECALL IT NOW AS A YEAR WHEN WE ACTUALLY had "seasons."

Definite "changes."

Changes not in the weather but in the caliber of the harmonic tremor.

I am not sure when everyone else realized that Antonio had diverted enough "secret" support from Victor's army to be finally immune from Victor but I know when I realized it. I realized it the evening Gerardo and Charlotte came back from Progreso and Charlotte began to cry at dinner.

"What upset her?" I said to Gerardo when Charlotte had left the table.

Gerardo was picking the meat from a crab and did not look at me.

"I suppose she didn't like Progreso," he said after a while. "I suppose she got tired. A day's outing. Very tiring."

"I said what upset her."

"I suppose she didn't find Progreso as peaceful as

you claim to." Gerardo placed the crabmeat as he picked it on Charlotte's plate. "I suppose it's a special taste."

"I want to know what upset her out there."

"M-3's," Charlotte said from the doorway.

She had washed her face clean of makeup and she seemed entirely composed.

"I grew up with shotguns but I can't stand carbines." She sat down and picked up her napkin. "Why are you staring at me?"

There was a silence.

"Whose carbines?" I said.

Gerardo avoided my eyes. "Grace hasn't been out to Progreso lately, Charlotte. Grace hasn't seen—what did you call it? Did you call it 'the machinery'?"

"I called it the hardware," Charlotte said.

"She calls it the hardware," Gerardo said.

"I don't have cancer of the ear," I said. "Whose hardware is it?"

"Antonio's got some of the army with him. Of course." Gerardo shrugged. The only clear evidence I have of Gerardo's intelligence is that he has always known how to cut his losses, yield the position, supply the information. Gerardo differs in that respect from Victor. "Actually it wasn't the guns that upset Charlotte. It was Antonio. Antonio and Carmen. Antonio gave Carmen an M-3 and let her shoot up the place."

Charlotte picked up her fork and laid it down again.

"You have a rather bizarre idea of a day's outing," I said to Gerardo.

"Carmen wasn't using an M-3," Charlotte said. She leaned forward slightly and her face was entirely grave. "Antonio was. Carmen was using an M-16."

Gerardo looked away.

"And they weren't shooting up 'the place,' Gerardo.

242

I mean what *is* 'the place.' 'The place' is some rusted cats and five flamingoes. They were only shooting the crates."

Something about Charlotte's querulous precision seemed extreme, and unnatural.

"What crates?" I said.

Charlotte looked at me.

"The crates of vaccine," she said. "The Lederle vaccine."

Charlotte never changed her expression.

"Unopened crates of Lederle vaccine," she said. "Cholera. It ran on the street when they shot up the crates."

I looked at her for a long time.

"It ran on the street," she repeated. "If you call that a street."

I think I loved Charlotte in that moment as a parent loves the child who has just fallen from a bicycle, met a pervert, lost a prize, come up in any way against the hardness of the world.

I think I was also angry at her, again like a parent, furious that she hadn't known better, furious that she had been wrong.

Tell Charlotte she was wrong.

What had Charlotte been wrong about exactly.

Who was wrong here.

I looked away from her.

"Why are you doing this with Antonio?" I said to Gerardo.

"I'm not 'doing' it, it's done. It's in progress. Underway. Its own momentum now."

"I know that," I said. "I want to know why you did it."

"It was something to do," Gerardo said.

"I happen to know about M–16s because Marin

243

had one when she went to Utah," Charlotte said. Charlotte always referred to the day Marin hijacked the L–1011 and burned it on the Bonneville Salt Flats as "when Marin went to Utah," as if it had been a tour of National Parks. Charlotte was not looking at me any more. "Or so they told me."

"Get her out before it happens," I said to Gerardo.

"The M–16 is supposed to be the 'ideal' submachine gun," Charlotte said. "Leonard called it ideal. They didn't."

"Tell me when it's time," I said to Gerardo.

"You always hear it," Gerardo said. "Eat that crab, Charlotte. I picked that crab for you."

I always did hear it.

I heard it because I listened.

Charlotte heard even more than I heard but Charlotte seemed not to listen.

Charlotte seemed not to see.

Charlotte had stood out there in the bamboo at Progreso and let the sun burn her face and heard Antonio call her *norteamericana cunt* and heard Carmen Arrellano call her *la bonne bourgeoise* and heard the carbine fire shatter the vials of clear American vaccine and still she did not listen. Charlotte had watched the clear American vaccine shimmer on the boulevards of Progreso and still she did not see.

That was August.

Boca Grande is.

Boca Grande was.

Boca Grande shall be.

11

LAND OF CONTRASTS.

Economic fulcrum of the Americas.

By the day in early September when Leonard Douglas finally arrived in Boca Grande it was clear that Victor was only playing for time. His couriers shuttled between Boca Grande and Geneva carrying heavy pouches. Military passes had been canceled. All day long Radio Boca Grande broadcast a single message, delivered by two voices, one male, one female, each threatening terrorists and saboteurs with death. It was clear that Victor would be leaving soon to convalesce in Bariloche. *El Presidente* had in fact already left to convalesce in Bariloche, omitting even the traditional move in which he first spends a week confined to the palace with a respiratory infection complicated by extreme exhaustion. Ardis Bradley had discovered a pressing need to take her children to Boston for school interviews. Tuck Bradley had stayed on but had twenty seats reserved on every flight leaving Boca Grande for any destination. I had two.

245

One for me.

One for Charlotte.

In other words.

All the markers were on the board.

"I'm Charlotte Douglas's husband," Leonard Douglas said to me.

"I know you are," I said to Leonard Douglas.

I knew that he had arrived in Boca Grande on one of the two or three flights that had managed to land the day before. He had gone directly to the Caribe and after a while he and Charlotte had been observed walking on the Avenida del Mar. It had been assumed that they were walking to her apartment but instead they had turned onto Calle 11 and entered the birth control clinic.

Victor had told me that.

Tuck Bradley had also told me that.

Gerardo had told me that he had no interest in Charlotte Douglas's former life.

"I wouldn't call yesterday her 'former life' exactly," I had said to Gerardo.

Gerardo had told me that I had too literal a mind.

Charlotte had told me nothing at all.

I got Leonard Douglas a drink.

He sat in my living room and drank it.

"I met your husband once," he said finally.

"He's dead now."

"I know that."

I got him another drink.

He put it on the table untouched.

"In Bogotá," he said. "I met him in Bogotá."

"When was that?"

"Before he died."

"Not after, then."

246

The acerbity in my voice went unnoticed.

"We had some business."

Leonard Douglas seemed absorbed in some contemplation of either Bogotá or Edgar, I did not know which.

I recall being uneasy.

"Where's Charlotte?" I said abruptly. "Did Charlotte send you to see me?"

"No." Leonard Douglas picked up the drink and put it down again. "I liked him. Your husband. I think he liked me. He gave me an emerald. As I was leaving. He gave me an emerald to take to Charlotte."

The square emerald.

The big square emerald Charlotte wore in place of a wedding ring.

The big square emerald Leonard had brought her from wherever he was when he met the man who financed the Tupamaros.

Bogotá.

Quito.

Charlotte had no idea whether it was Bogotá or Quito.

It was Bogotá.

I had no idea.

I prided myself on listening and seeing and I had never even heard or seen that Edgar played the same games Gerardo played.

Leonard Douglas was watching me.

"Why did you tell me that," I said finally.

"I wanted you to know that I understand what's going on here."

"Why."

"Because," Leonard Douglas said, "I want you to get Charlotte out."

"It could be smooth," I said after a while. I did not believe that it would be smooth. "Sometimes it's smooth."

"It's not going to be smooth," Leonard Douglas said.

"How do you know."

"I don't want you to think I'm involved here."

"Nobody said you were."

"I want you to believe me." Leonard Douglas seemed to tense as he spoke. "I have no interest here."

"I believe you."

As a matter of fact I did believe him.

I also believed him about Edgar.

I still do.

It still disturbs me and I still believe him.

"It's not going to be smooth," he repeated. "I'm not involved but I hear things."

I said nothing.

"I hear there's more outside hardware than there's supposed to be. You know what I mean."

I did know what he meant.

He meant that someone had outplayed Gerardo and Antonio.

He meant that the *guerrilleros* were not going to just serve their purpose and get gunned down on the fourth day by an insurgent army under Antonio's command.

He meant that for a certain number of days or weeks no one at all could be certain of knowing the right people in Boca Grande.

"So get her out," he said finally.

"Why don't you take her out?"

"She won't go with me."

"Why not?"

Leonard Douglas sat for a while and ran his finger around the rim of his glass.

"She remembers everything," he said after a while. And then. "You met Warren Bogart."

It was a question.

"Once. In New Orleans. He said he was dying."

"Yes. Well." Leonard Douglas looked suddenly exhausted. "He was right."

12

"WHO WAS THERE," CHARLOTTE HAD SAID WHEN Leonard told her that Warren Bogart was dead.

As he sat in my living room and told me what she had said he kept repeating the words as if he could not believe them: *who was there.*

He remembered that she said it at the corner of Avenida del Mar and Calle 11.

He had come to Boca Grande to tell her three things.

He had come to tell her that certain of his former clients had put him in touch with someone in the underground who had put him in touch with Marin.

He had come to tell her to get out of Boca Grande.

He had come to tell her that he had buried Warren Bogart a few days before in New Orleans.

He told her none of these things until they were out of the Caribe and walking on the Avenida del Mar where they could not be heard.

He told her that Marin was living with six other people in a semi-detached house in the industrial section of Buffalo and she said nothing at all. She began

to cry and she kept on walking and she said nothing
at all. He told her to get out of Boca Grande and she
said nothing at all. She folded and refolded the piece
of paper he had given her with the number of the post-
office box in Buffalo and she said nothing at all. He
told her that he had buried Warren Bogart and she
walked until they reached the corner of Avenida del
Mar and Calle 11 and as they turned the corner onto
Calle 11 she said something. He remembered that he
had just realized that she was walking not idly but
toward a specific destination and then she said something.

She said *who was there*.

"I told you. He was alone. He'd been in and out of
Ochsner for a month and this time he just walked
out without anybody knowing and he was alone on the
street. And he collapsed. And they took him to Long
Memorial and they put him on life-support but he
never woke up."

"Who was there."

"Charlotte. No one was there. He had a letter in
his coat with the number on California Street. Your
number and Porter's number. They tried to get Porter
and they couldn't. Porter was in New York. They tried
to get you and they got me. He was on the machine
for the rest of the day and he died before I got there."

"Who was there," Charlotte repeated. "When he was
buried. You said you buried him. *Who came*."

"I got hold of Porter. Porter came."

She seemed to be waiting for something.

"A couple of people I didn't know."

She still seemed to be waiting for something.

"And six FBI."

She had stopped in front of a building on Calle 11
and still she seemed to be waiting.

"It was fine, Charlotte. He didn't want anyone there. The letter said so. The letter they found in his coat. All he wanted was nobody there and somebody singing 'Didn't I Ramble.' "

Charlotte said nothing.

The letter in Warren Bogart's coat also had a message for Charlotte and Marin but Leonard did not mention the message.

"He carried it in his coat. The letter." Leonard shook his head. "He did. Didn't he."

"He did what."

"He did ramble."

The message for Charlotte and Marin had read only *you were both wrong but it's all the same in the end* and Leonard did not mention the message.

"Not a letter really," he said. "A note. On the back of an envelope."

"This is where I work," Charlotte said. "I'm quite late now."

She looked directly at Leonard as she spoke and then she turned and walked inside and down a corridor and into an office. When he followed her into the office she was standing at the window smoking a cigarette and staring out at the blank wall of the adjoining building and she did not turn around.

"Would you go to the desk for me," she said after a while. She did not turn from the window. "Would you tell them I can't see anyone for a few minutes. Twenty minutes."

"I'll call." Leonard picked up the telephone and jiggled it. "How do you call?"

"You don't. The switchboard's out. Or something. Since the bomb."

He stared at her.

"You had a bomb here?"

252

"Or something."

"When was the bomb? Or something."

"I don't know. Yesterday. No, it was the day before, because I still had the curse, I was changing a Tampax when it went off. Would you please go to the desk?"

Leonard put the telephone down and watched Charlotte crush her cigarette on the ledge outside the window.

"I want you to come with me," he said after a while. "I never told you what to do but I'm telling you now. I want you to come with me to the airport. Now."

"Actually I can't," Charlotte said, and then she turned abruptly from the window. *"Didn't Marin come."*

"She couldn't have, Charlotte. I told you. The FBI were there. Naturally the FBI were there."

"Did you tell Marin."

"Yes."

"Did she want to come."

There was a silence.

"I don't know," Leonard said.

"Tell her she was wrong," Charlotte said. "Tell her that for me."

13

"AND WHAT ABOUT THIS FUCKING BOMB," LEONARD Douglas said to me.

He had finally drunk his second drink and then a third and a fourth. He was in no way drunk but he gave off the sense of a man who normally had one drink, maybe two when politesse required it, a man who prized control and had been pushed in a single week almost beyond it.

He had found Marin Bogart in an empty room in Buffalo.

He had buried Warren Bogart in an empty grave in New Orleans.

He had come to save Charlotte from an empty revolution in Boca Grande and Charlotte was not listening.

He had found his way to me and and in my house there were flowers in the vases and ice cubes in the carafes and clean uniforms on the maids. In my house it did not seem so empty and I was listening.

" 'A bomb or something,' she says. Don't miss the *or*

something. I look around, I discover the back wing of the building blew up three days ago, I find four people died outright and the fifth's dying now, peritonitis, this fifth one got caught on the table, the doctor jumped and punctured this one's fucking—"

Leonard Douglas seemed to have rendered himself temporarily mute.

"Uterus," I said. "I heard there was a bomb. Before you came. I asked Charlotte about it. Charlotte said—"

I broke off. Charlotte had said that when the bomb went off she was in the bathroom and she had forgotten about her Tampax and had spotted blood all over the clinic without realizing it.

That was all she had said.

"She said it wasn't near her office," I said.

"Never mind where it *wasn't.* Because she goes charging in where it *was,* the ceiling's still falling, she gets three people out, she's a heroine, she's mad as hell, she's shouting '*Goddamn you all*' the whole time. *They* tell me that. *Charlotte* doesn't. All Charlotte remembers about this bomb is it went off while she was changing her fucking Tampax."

"She bled." I did not know what else to say. "She remembers she bled all over the clinic."

Leonard Douglas looked at me a long while.

He loosened his tie and closed his eyes.

It was just sundown and I could hear the DDT truck outside.

"Yeah," he said finally. "She remembers she bled."

The DDT truck was gone before he spoke again.

"You didn't know about Bogotá, did you."

"No."

"I shouldn't have told you. It upset you."

"I should have known."

"She should have known too." Leonard Douglas stood up and picked up his jacket. He did not seem to be talking to me at all. "It wasn't the way she thought it was either. I wasn't the way she thought I was and Marin wasn't the way she thought Marin was and Warren wasn't the way she thought Warren was. She didn't know any of us."

"She remembers everything," I said. "You said she remembers everything."

"No," Leonard Douglas said. "She remembers she bled."

14

A FEW DAYS AFTER LEONARD DOUGLAS LEFT BOCA Grande Charlotte told me that he had "passed through" but had left before she could "arrange an evening" for him.

"An 'evening,' " I remember saying. An evening for a man who had just found her child and buried her child's father. An evening for such a man in an equatorial city under martial law and rigid curfew. "What kind of 'evening' exactly did you have in mind?"

"An evening to meet everyone. Of course. I particularly wanted him to meet you."

"He did meet me," I said after a while. "He spent three hours here in this room. He told me about Marin. He told me about Warren."

She looked away before she spoke.

"I know he did," she said. "I don't want to talk about it."

Charlotte stood up then and walked out onto the terrace and across the lawn to where the roses grew. I remembered her walking across the lawn the night she met Gerardo and I remembered Elena and I remembered Ardis Bradley and I remembered Carmen Arrellano and I wished suddenly that Charlotte had gone to Paris.

You smell American.

I wonder what American smells like exactly.

Norteamericana cunt.

When Charlotte came back inside she did not look at me.

When Charlotte came back she was already talking and her voice was low.

Charlotte wondered if she had ever told me about the night Marin was born. Marin was born at Flower-Fifth Avenue Hospital in New York. Warren hit the head nurse on the maternity floor. The head nurse brought assault charges but later dropped them. Marin weighed six-eight at birth but only six-two by the time they took her home. Charlotte supposed that was normal. Warren was afraid to hold Marin in the taxi going home. Charlotte supposed he had been drinking. Instead of holding Marin he held his hands an inch or so above the soft spot on her head to protect it if the taxi bumped and he said over and over again that he did not want her to go to Smith and marry some eighth-rate ass from Sullivan and Cromwell.

"And I don't guess she ever will," Charlotte said finally. Her voice was devoid of expression. "I guess he got that wish."

There was a silence.

"Now you can see her," I said.

"No," Charlotte said. "I can't exactly."

"But you know how to reach her."

"She's always known how to reach me," Charlotte said. "If you want to look at it that way."

I said nothing.

"So in the first place it's not even Marin."

I think she meant that it was not the Marin she remembered.

There was nothing to say.

"Marin would have found Warren. Marin would have found me."

Tell Marin she was wrong. Tell her that for me.

Goddamn you all.

She remembers she bled.

15

ON THE AFTERNOON I WENT TO THE CARIBE TO TELL
Charlotte that she and I were leaving for New Orleans,
that the last planes were getting out, that Tuck Bradley
was closing the Embassy, Charlotte only shook her
head.

"Not just yet," she said.

She was sitting in the lobby of the Caribe staring at
a television screen which for days had shown only the
emblem of La República de Boca Grande, with military music played over the emblem.

"Charlotte. Look at me. You plan to wait until they
announce it on television?"

"I just want to see what happens."

"All that happens is that people get hurt. People get
killed. You're maybe going to get killed if you stay
here."

"Don't be operatic, Grace, I'm not staying here. I'm
just not leaving tonight."

I said nothing.

"In the first place I don't like New Orleans. In the

second place, take my word for it, it's going to be a very tedious flight with Tuck Bradley aboard. Carrying his flag."

"Charlotte. I'm going tonight."

"Of course you are. Remember to tell Tuck when you land, he's supposed to get off with the flag showing. Folded. Under his arm. But *showing*."

"I promised Leonard I'd take you out with me."

"*I* promised Leonard." Her voice was all gentle reproach and I never heard the steel in it until after she was dead. "I promised I'd see him very soon. There was no call for him to worry you. We talked about it."

She was still gazing at the television screen.

"In any case you're not to worry," she said without looking up. "I told Leonard what I was going to do."

I had asked Victor to make her leave and Victor had said he had no authority.

I had asked Gerardo to make her leave and Gerardo had said he would get her out.

I had asked Antonio to make her leave and Antonio had said *norteamericana cunt*.

Before I left for the airport that night Charlotte came to the house with presents for my trip: a travel-sized vial of Grès perfume, a gardenia for my dress, and all the latest magazines and papers. She was on her way to the Jockey Club for dinner.

16

IN FACT SHE HAD.

Told Leonard what she was going to do.

She was going to stay.

Not "stay" precisely.

"Not leave" is more like it.

"I walked away from places all my life and I'm not going to walk away from here," is exactly what she said to him.

She had said it to him at the clinic and she had said it to him at the Caribe and she had said it to him for the last time the night he left, while they waited for his flight to get clearance out.

I did not know the exact words until after she was dead.

I walked away from places all my life and I'm not going to walk away from here.

"You have to pick the places you don't walk away from," Leonard had said that night at the airport.

The waiting room was empty and the runways were lit up with crossfire from the hardware that the *guerrilleros* were not supposed to have had. "This isn't one of those places. It's the wrong place, Charlotte."

"I think that's a song," Charlotte had said. " 'The wrong place, the right face'? Is that how it goes?"

"Charlotte—"

"Sing it for me. No." She touched his lips with her fingers. "You have a terrible voice. Tell me about the terrific dinner we're going to have the next time we're in Paris."

"What about Marin."

"Get that big suite at the Plaza Athénée."

"Marin wants to see you."

"And get—she didn't say that. Did she."

Leonard said nothing.

Charlotte took Leonard's hand and she kissed each finger, very lightly, very precisely.

"I knew she didn't say that," she said then. "Another thing I knew, I knew you wouldn't lie to me. You lie for a living but you never lie to me."

"You don't get any real points for staying here, Charlotte."

"I can't seem to tell what you do get the real points for," Charlotte said. "So I guess I'll stick around here awhile."

And when his plane was cleared to leave she had walked out to the gate with him and he had said again *don't you want to see Marin* and she had said *I don't have to see Marin because I have Marin in my mind and Marin has me in her mind* and they closed the gate and that was the last time Leonard Douglas ever saw Charlotte alive.

* * *

A BOOK OF COMMON PRAYER

The last time I ever saw Charlotte alive was the night two weeks later when I left for New Orleans.

When she pinned her gardenia on my dress.

When she dabbed her Grès perfume on my wrists.

Like a child helping her mother dress for a party.

17

I don't have to see Marin because I have Marin in my mind.

I don't have to see Marin because Marin has me in her mind.

In that dirty room in Buffalo those seemed increasingly ambiguous propositions.

"All right," I said finally to Marin Bogart. "You tell me. You tell *me* what you think your mother did in Boca Grande."

"I think she played tennis all day," Marin Bogart said.

"She didn't ever play tennis," I said.

"All day. Every day. I only remember her in a tennis dress."

"I never saw her in a tennis dress."

As a matter of fact Charlotte had told me that she and Marin once modeled matching tennis dresses in a fashion show at the Burlingame Country Club and that because she did not play tennis she had needed to ask Marin how to hold the racquet correctly.

265

"I'm quite sure your mother didn't play tennis," I said.

"She always wore a tennis dress," Marin Bogart said.

"More than once?"

"Always."

"Didn't you play tennis?"

"Tennis," Marin Bogart said, "is just one more mode of teaching an elitist strategy. If you subject it to a revolutionary analysis you'll see that. Not that I think you will."

We sat facing each other in the bleak room.

You were both wrong but it's all the same in the end.

We all remember what we need to remember.

Marin remembered Charlotte in a tennis dress and Charlotte remembered Marin in a straw hat for Easter. I remembered Edgar, I did not remember Edgar as the man who financed the Tupamaros. Charlotte remembered she bled. I remembered the light in Boca Grande. I sat in this room in Buffalo where I had no business being and I talked to this child who was not mine and I remembered the light in Boca Grande.

Another place I have no business being.

It seems to me now.

"Why did you bother agreeing to see me?" I said finally.

"My stepfather said he was putting you in touch with me because you had something important to tell me. I can see you don't."

I remember feeling ill and trying to control my dislike of Charlotte's child.

"I didn't understand your mother," I said finally.

"Try a class analysis."

I had not come ill to Buffalo to scream at Charlotte's child. "Your mother disturbed me," I said.

"She could certainly do that."

I tried again. "She had you in her mind. She always kept you in her mind."

"Not me," Marin Bogart said. "Some pretty baby. Not me."

"Could I have a glass of water," I said after a while.

"We don't have liquor."

"I didn't ask for liquor. Did I." I could hear the fury in my voice and could not stop. "I didn't ask for 'liquor' and I didn't ask for 'diet pills' and I didn't ask for Saran Wrap and I didn't ask for white bread and I didn't ask for any of the other things I'm sure you make it a point not to have. I asked for a glass of water."

Marin Bogart watched me without expression for a moment and then stood up and turned to the sink full of dirty dishes.

"Did you like the Tivoli Gardens," I said suddenly.

"This water runs lukewarm. I better get you some ice, this is lukewarm water and I can at least get you some ice, can't I."

As she spoke she opened the refrigerator and took out an ice tray. Her movements were jerky and the tray was not frozen and the water splashed on the floor.

"I said did you like the Tivoli Gardens."

"God*damn* people around here, somebody took it out last night and never put it back, I mean *I* had to put it back this morning, I don't think—"

She was speaking very rapidly and for the first time something other than her eyes reminded me of Charlotte.

"—Anyone but me ever raises a finger around here, I honestly—"

"Tivoli," I said.

Marin Bogart turned suddenly, and she put the tray on the table, and her face was tight, and then she broke exactly as her mother must have broken the morning the FBI first came to the house on California Street.

SIX

IN THE END THERE WAS NOT MUCH TO TELL MARIN Bogart that she could understand and there was even less to tell Leonard Douglas that he could not have guessed.

It did not go smoothly at all.

Since I was in New Orleans I know only a few facts.

Since I do not entirely trust Gerardo's version of it I am certain of even fewer facts.

On the first day of what has come to be remembered as the October Violence the *guerrilleros* finally closed the airport altogether.

The final closing of the airport is what we usually call Day One.

I had flown out the night before, the evening of the day we usually call Day Minus One. I lost the gardenia in the crush at the airport.

The seat next to mine on the plane out was empty.

Charlotte was eating spiny lobster at the Jockey Club.

Day Minus One. Day One.

Day Two.

On Day Two the *guerrilleros* took over the radio stations.

On Day Three the *guerrilleros* neared the palace.

Those first three days went more or less as expected.

I have seen the troops on the palace roof waiting to pick off the *guerrilleros* before.

It was Day Four which did not go as planned. Day Four is supposed to end just after the heavy shooting at dawn, but this time it did not. The *guerrilleros* appeared not to know that they were on the board only to be gunned down at dawn of Day Four by the insurgent army under Antonio's "new leadership." The *guerrilleros* appeared to have more of everything than anyone except Leonard Douglas had supposed they had. Some say Kasindorf and Riley supplied the excess, some say other agencies. Some say Victor.

I think not Victor but have no empirical proof.

I also think (still) that Leonard Douglas was not involved but again this conclusion is not empirical.

In any case.

2

GERARDO HAD COUNTED ON A SMOOTH TRANSITION.

Gerardo had counted on dinner at the Jockey Club the evening of Day Four.

By Day Seven Gerardo wanted to get out himself.

"I couldn't possibly leave right now," Charlotte said when Gerardo told her about the helicopter in Millon-ario.

"You don't realize," Gerardo said.

"I realize," Charlotte said. "I do realize."

"Charlotte. You don't leave now, you're not going to leave at all, because Antonio wants Carmen Arrellano on that chopper and not you."

"Then take Carmen Arrellano. Carmen should get out, Carmen has connections here."

"So do you."

"No." Charlotte had seemed vague and distant. "I don't actually."

"Charlotte. *Remember Victor. Remember me.*"

And Charlotte had looked at Gerardo for a while and smiled as she sometimes smiled at strangers.

"I wasn't connected to you actually," Charlotte had said.

Gerardo had only stared at her.

"I mean I've got two or three people in my mind but I don't quite have you."

I trust Gerardo's version on this point.

I wasn't connected to you actually has the ring of Charlotte Douglas to me.

DAY EIGHT.

There had never been a Day Eight in Boca Grande before.

On Day Eight Charlotte appeared to have gone as usual to the clinic. She was reported to have stayed in her office all day but of course there would have been no callers for birth control devices on Day Eight. At five o'clock she closed the clinic and walked to the Caribe and apparently changed for dinner. At any rate she was wearing a clean linen dress when she left the Caribe at seven-thirty and began to walk in the direction of the Capilla del Mar.

Walking very deliberately.

Tying and retying a scarf which whipped in the hot night wind.

Seeming to concentrate on the scarf as if oblivious to the potholes in the sidewalk and the places where waste ran into the gutters.

At seven-forty-three exactly she reached the bar-

ricade on the sidewalk outside the Capilla del Mar and
she stopped and she showed her passport.

Soy norteamericana, she said.

Soy una turista, she said.

The passport was knocked from her hand by the
butt of a carbine.

"Don't you lay your fucking hands on me," she said
in English.

Goddamn you all.

She was taken to the Escuela de los Niños Perdidos
and detained overnight before she was transferred to
the Estadio Nacional for interrogation. The moment
and circumstances of her arrest are matters of record
but the moment and circumstances of her death remain
obscure. I do not even know which side killed her,
who held the Estadio Nacional at the moment of death.
I know that fire from either an AR–15 or an AR–16
entered her body just below the left shoulder-blade
but I also know that all sides had both weapons.

Other than that I know only what Gerardo told me.

That she cried not for God but for Marin.

"She was shot in the back," I said to Gerardo.

"Maybe she wanted to have it that way," Gerardo
said.

"She wouldn't have wanted to have it that way."

"Well," Gerardo said, "she did."

That Gerardo knew she cried for Marin suggests
that Antonio was in charge of the Estadio Nacional
at the moment of death but there are no real points in
knowing one way or another.

As Leonard Douglas might say.

As Leonard Douglas did say, when I told him.

I no longer know where the real points are.

I am more like Charlotte than I thought I was.

On the day Antonio finally managed to take over

Victor's office the October Violence ended. On the day after that Victor flew back from Bariloche, I flew back from New Orleans, and Charlotte Douglas's body was found, where it had been thrown, on the lawn of the American Embassy. Since all Embassy personnel had abandoned the building the point was lost on them.

Although not on me.

And possibly not even on Victor.

Norteamericana cunt.

4

ALL I CAN TELL YOU DIRECTLY ABOUT CHARLOTTE Douglas's death is that I sent her body to San Francisco. I had the body put in a coffin and I went to the airport with the coffin and I waited there until I could see, for myself, the coffin loaded into the hold of the first Pan American flight to leave Boca Grande after the October Violence. I wanted to lay a flag on the coffin but there were no American flags in Boca Grande that week and in the end I bought a child's T-shirt in the gift shop at the airport. This T-shirt was printed like an American flag. I dropped this T-shirt on the coffin as it was loaded into the hold of the Boeing. I think this T-shirt did not have the correct number of stars or stripes but it did have the appearance of stars and stripes and it was red and it was white and it was blue. There were no real points in that either.

5

IN SUMMARY.

So you know the story.

Today we are clearing some coastal groves by slash-and-burn and a pall of smoke hangs over Boca Grande. The smoke colors everything. The smoke obscures the light. You will notice my use of the colonial pronoun, the overseer's "we." I mean it. I see now that I have no business in this place but I have been here too long to change. I mean "we." I wish that I could see the light today but I recognize the necessity for clearing groves. I also recognize the equivocal nature of even the most empirical evidence. Some evidence I did not know about until quite recently, when crates of mail uncollected during the October Violence that year were located and distributed. The evidence came to me long after I had talked to Leonard Douglas and been put in touch with Marin Bogart in Buffalo. This evidence came to me long after I had seen Marin Bogart in Buffalo. Here it is. Early on the evening of her arrest, from a box between the Caribe and the Capilla del

A BOOK OF COMMON PRAYER

Mar, Charlotte Douglas mailed me Marin's address. She also mailed me the big square emerald she wore in place of a wedding ring. I wrote to Marin and told her I have the emerald but have received no reply. I did not mention to Marin that the emerald was a memento from the man who financed the Tupamaros.

Marin has no interest in the past.

I still do, but understand it no better.

All I know now is that when I think of Charlotte Douglas walking in the hot night wind toward the lights at the Capilla del Mar I am less and less certain that this story has been one of delusion.

Unless the delusion was mine.

When I am tired I remember what I was taught in Colorado. On Day Minus One in Boca Grande Charlotte remembered to bring me a gardenia for my trip. Her mother taught her that. Marin and I are inseparable. She had a straw hat one Easter, and a flowered lawn dress. Tell Charlotte she was wrong. Tell Marin she was wrong. Tell her that for me. She remembers everything. She remembers she bled. The wind is up and I will die and rather soon and all I know empirically is *I am told*.

I am told, and so she said.

I heard later.

According to her passport. It was reported.

Apparently.

I have not been the witness I wanted to be.

280

Fine Fiction By
TOP WOMEN WRITERS

Novels that speak to women's needs,
desires, problems.
Novels about women who are sensitive,
talented, demanding and ready for anything.
Great new novels <u>by</u> women <u>for</u> women
who are not afraid to ask for what they want.